THEN, THERE

STORIES

Hugo dos Santos

SPUYTEN DUYVIL
NEW YORK CITY

Acknowledgments

The author is grateful to the editors of those periodicals where other versions of the following stories first appeared:

"Avô" in *Barrelhouse*; "Borders" in *Hinchas de Poesia*; "Night" in *Hobart*; "Passage" in *Lunch Ticket*; "Outside in" in *Queen Mob's Tea House*; "Robin moved in" and "The day my father decided to die" in *Brittle Star*, "Wisdom" in *The Common*

Library of Congress Cataloging-in-Publication Data

Names: Santos, Hugo dos, 1980- author.
Title: Then, there : stories / Hugo dos Santos.
Description: New York City : Spuyten Duyvil, [2019]
Identifiers: LCCN 2018045033 | ISBN 9781947980945
Subjects: LCSH: Newark (N.J.)--Fiction.
Classification: LCC PS3619.A5968 A6 2019 | DDC 813/.6--dc23
LC record available at https://lccn.loc.gov/2018045033

for Lucas

Janelas do meu quarto,
Do meu quarto de um dos milhões do mundo que ninguém sabe quem é
(E se soubessem quem é, o que saberiam?),
Dais para o mistério de uma rua cruzada constantemente por gente,
Para uma rua inacessível a todos os pensamentos

— Fernando Pessoa, "A Tabacaria"

BORDERS

The Ms went to church regularly, but not every Sunday. And during the summer sometimes they didn't go at all. We went every Sunday at the same time, year-round, and we prayed every night before bed, which we knew the Ms didn't do. We had named our guardian angels. We were closer to God than the Ms.

It's not enough to just be good, our father said. We have to combat evil, he added. He said it just like that. Combat, which I remember because it sounded weird to me back then. That word. Combat.

We were at the kitchen table and I looked at the door that led to the landing we shared with the Ms.

We have to combat the evil, our father said that night, as our mother cleared away the dishes. My brother and I looked at one another and nodded.

— // — // —

The Ms started doing many things that were very evil.

One thing they did that was evil, they used small plastic bags from the supermarket for their garbage. They didn't tie the bags properly and there would be a mess everywhere, all over the sidewalk stinking up the street in front of our apartment building.

Another thing they did, they watched movies with the tv very loud. We could hear it in the hallway.

At first we liked the Ms. When they moved in our mother talked to their mother in the stairwell. My brother and I played in our room and heard them talking but we never paid attention to what they said. They would be out there for a long time, on the landing. Sometimes one hour. One time they were out there longer than that, each with a laundry basket on her hip, just talking.

I walked out there and asked our mother if she was ok.

Yes, our mother said. I am just talking to Mrs. M. Did you say hello?

Hello, I said.

I'll be right in, our mother said with a knowing smile. I went back to playing. I didn't hate the Ms back then.

The Ms had a son and a daughter. The son was older than my brother, so he was older than me too. He was weird and only had a few friends at school and then came straight home. The daughter was younger than me, so she was younger than my brother too.

She had her hair in a ponytail and wore lots of hair spray. She had a gold ring with her name on it.

We never spoke to her.

They walked home from school together and promptly locked the door to their apartment. They never played outside, not even in the summer.

The Ms did not care about where they lived. They made this clear in several ways.

One thing they did that showed they didn't care, they never vacuumed. We never heard a vacuum in their apartment.

Another thing they did, they sometimes left the front door open to the street, with the deadbolt turned to keep the door from closing all the way. I tried to catch them doing this, several times, because I was sure it was them and I wanted to tell them how wrong this was. If I had caught them in the act, I might have only said something very small even though I really wanted to say many things. But I would have given them a look that meant as much and they would have known.

I never caught them. Each time I closed the door properly and hoped they would be stuck outside so they could learn a lesson.

— // — // —

The Ms had no friends. They never had anyone over. They were very unfriendly people.

— // — // —

Over the summer, the Ms put up a flag on the door to their apartment. This was right after the World Cup. The flag hung down from the top and covered almost the entire door. It was blue and white and red.

That night, our father asked us if we had seen the flag.

My brother and I both said yes, though I had been the first to see it.

This is unbelievable, our father said. They don't care about where they live. Who ever heard of putting a flag on a door?

— // — // —

The next morning, after our father and mother had gone to their jobs, I waited for my brother to go into the bathroom. I took the scissors from the kitchen drawer and I walked up to the Ms' door and I cut a small piece off their flag.

I knew the Ms were gone, I had heard them going down the stairs when they left, all four of them together, so I didn't have to worry about being caught. I cut a triangle from the bottom left corner and I put the triangle of fabric in my pocket like a trophy and walked back inside our apartment.

Then I worried that I would be caught so I hid the fabric in the drawer where my brother kept his underwear.

— // — // —

In church, we learned about the importance of repenting for sins.

At the dinner table that night, our father asked us whether we had thought about the sermon.

I said yes.

My brother nodded.

I thought of many things the Ms had done wrong.

One thing they had done wrong, they sometimes didn't go to church.

Another thing they did, they made weird foods that made the landing we shared with them outside our apartment smell for days. I had heard that people from where the Ms were from even ate cow tongues and pig heads.

Another thing they did, they watched movies with the tv even louder than before.

My father was very upset about it. He told my mother that if they kept playing the tv so loud one day he would go and knock down their door.

— // — // —

Later that year, when the weather got cold, the Ms started drying laundry in the landing we shared with them. They set up a rack right outside their door, a mere ten feet from the door to our apartment, and they hung everything from socks to dresses on that rack. And once those clothes dried the Ms took them inside and put out other clothes to dry. It got so bad that we couldn't walk in or out of our apartment or go to sleep or watch tv without clothes out there drying on the landing.

The third floor neighbors would walk by on their way in and out and they would see that mess out there, right at our door.

It was so embarrassing. I hated the Ms.

— // — // —

My brother and I decided that something had to be done. One day, as we were leaving for school, we grabbed one of the dresses drying on the rack. It was garbage day, so we threw it in one of the gray garbage pails on the curb. We tried our best to hide it under some of the bags but we didn't want to touch the garbage too much. We ran the rest of the way, partly euphoric partly nervous we'd get caught. We laughed so hard.

At night we told our mother what we had done.

Her eyes got very big and she asked us why we had done it.

I said, To teach them a lesson.

— // — // —

A few weeks later the Ms added another rack. The weather was brutal at this point and it seemed like it was snowing every night but they were still dirtying clothes and washing them and drying them on our landing. It was so bad that from our doorway I had only to take one step and stretch out my arm to touch one of the racks.

It's too close, our father said. Every time we walk in we have to look at their longjohns?

I never saw a family dirty so many clothes, our mother said.

Our father said they had no respect. Watch out for people like that, he said. That's why it's so important for you to learn proper manners, he said to me and my brother, though he looked more intently at me. Those people are miserables, he said.

We didn't even say hello to the Ms when we saw them in the street or at the supermarket or school.

— // — // —

One morning that winter, after a really bad snow storm closed the school for three days, we helped our father clear out his car by digging out the spot where he was parked on our street so he could go to work. There was snow everywhere and no place to put it. It took us two hours to finish but we had fun. After our father pulled out we blocked the spot with a bucket and a plank of wood we had found in the basement of our building.

My brother and I looked at our work and threw snow at each other and then we went inside with our mother.

When our father came home from work that evening he found another car parked in the spot we had cleared. Someone had moved the bucket and the plank of wood and parked in the spot we had cleared. Our father had to drive around for 35 minutes before finally finding an open spot three blocks away.

At the kitchen table we watched our father eat and he told us about what happened to him and explained how a small white car with tinted windows had taken our spot.

That's the Ms' car, I said.

Our father and mother looked at each other.

Yeah, my brother added. I saw them going in that car last week.

— // — // —

Over the next few weeks, I looked for the Ms' car everywhere. I even volunteered to run to the corner store for my mother a few times hoping I would find it. Walking to and from school, I kept my keys ready just in case.

— // — // —

At some point I realized that the Ms spoke a different kind of E than we did. I had always just thought it was their accent but some of the words they used weren't words at all, just made up names for things that had proper names if only the Ms spoke proper E.

I knew where they were from and that they had left there less than one year before, but I had never noticed how silly their speaking was. Once I realized it, I noticed it every time they and other people like them talked.

People that speak that kind of way have no respect. We knew that. Everyone in the neighborhood knew that. Those people had crazy haircuts. They wore their jeans low and their shirts loose and a good number of them were liars and cheaters. Criminals. The Ms had seemed different to us at first, like maybe they weren't like most of their kind. But then we realized that we had been wrong. Then we realized that they had tricked us.

— // — // —

One time, as I was coming back from the corner store with a bag of potatoes, I saw the Ms, all four of them, come out of the front door and head in the opposite direction. They didn't see me so I followed them, hiding between cars and being very careful. I hoped I would see their car at last.

They stopped at the corner and when a bus came a few minutes later they got in. I didn't get to see their car.

— // — // —

One Saturday afternoon when the snow on the street was starting to melt, the Ms were watching their tv really loud and our father got very mad and sent my brother to knock on their door and tell them that their tv was too loud.

My brother came back and said that the Ms had said ok but then their tv was even louder so our father called the police and told them that the Ms had their tv too loud.

My brother and I put our ears to the door when we heard the police coming up the stairs and knocking on the Ms' door. My father said Shh. There was talking on the landing and then the police left and the tv was lower. Then it got loud again, really loud, louder than ever and our father was getting ready to send our mother to talk to the Ms when we heard a scream.

It was a scream to stop everything. I'm sure everyone heard it, from the first floor all the way to the third. We waited. Their tv was still loud but the scream had been louder so we were waiting for an explanation since we knew there were only a few things that could cause a scream of that kind. Then there were people coming up the stairs and there was more talking outside our door and we heard Mrs. M and it sounded like she was crying.

From our window, we saw an ambulance outside. We heard more talking in the landing. Then there was walking down the stairs and it sounded like people were carrying something heavy because we kept hearing instructions like Let's go really slow and Let's put him down for a second and He's falling off the side and We're ok, it's ok, hold on, ok, come on, one more step.

Their tv went off and there was a ringing in the air like when you're all alone and it's really quiet.

We heard someone locking the Ms' door and there was a really loud bang at our door. Our father made his eyes very big and put his right index finger to his mouth. I remember, it was his right index finger. We were in the kitchen very quiet looking at each other.

There was a loud bang again as if someone had a large hammer and had pounded our door with it. Then there was a scream loud like the one we had heard before, but this one was deeper and scared us because it was much bigger than our door. I couldn't imagine how a scream like that could fit in the landing. We looked at my father's finger again for guidance. We waited.

Then steps ran down the stairs and slammed the front door shut.

We opened our door and looked out into the landing. The racks were on the floor, off to the side by the stairs leading up to the floor above, and there were clothes on the floor too.

— // — // —

The Ms changed after that.

One thing they did that was a change, they took away the racks, though the weather was nicer now and I know they were drying clothes in the line outside their windows.

Another thing they did, we never heard their tv again.

Father said, some people have to be taught a lesson. Look at the Ms, they learned. You have to do the right thing.

— // — // —

One Sunday, coming home from church, I asked our father about ghosts. Are they real?

Of course not, he said, turning the key to the front door.

Our mother made lunch and while we were at the table we heard three sets of steps walk out of the Ms' apartment and down the stairs.

Ghosts aren't real, he said. I don't believe in ghosts.

— // — // —

By that summer the Ms were gone. Another family moved in but we never talked to them and they never talked to us. They spoke our kind of E and their kids were very young.

They were different.

One thing they did that was different, they had a vacuum.

Another thing they did, we never heard their tv.

Another thing they did, in the fall, they started coming to our church.

PASSAGE

As a girl of seven, she was told to pretend the stranger was her father. Fake passports and stories to match, enough to fool inquisitive Customs officers. At first, she'd wondered whether going to America meant she'd get a different father. A father who was there, not just a name to put to a framed picture in the living room. And then, outside the Departures terminal, was that what an American father looked like — younger and in a denim jacket? She memorized his birthdate, the color of his eyes. He complimented her for being such a smart girl. She remembered it still: his hand on her shoulder, his comforting nods to her mother. He was a ghost that remained with her; a shadow longer than a promise. Sometimes in the shower, trying to come after a long day at work, her unguarded mind would land on her mind's portrait of his face. Something about his heavy eyes, conveying a belief certain as an anchor. After all these years she remembered how he had said her name. He'd been the first to pronounce it in the Anglicized syllables she later came to identify with herself. A milky glaze drizzled over the delivery. The softer R, an easy roll over the first A. It had all started with him, the doors and life and existence that formed her now as much as that birthing Portuguese village faded behind yellowed curtains of hovering dirt. A fake father was all it took to come to America. After the flight and the questions and the suitcases, he disappeared into a cab and she was back to being someone else's daughter.

NIGHT

On November 13, 2012, Hugo Dos Santos woke up shortly after 1 am with an urgent need to urinate. He got up from bed and took two steps out into the hallway when he saw three small creatures in surgical masks and lab coats, each no more than two feet tall, engaged in some kind of group preparation outside his son's bedroom. His first instinct was to protect his boy, and he was momentarily proud of his reaction, but the creatures were much stronger than their size would suggest. They easily wrestled him facedown to the dark oak floor and pinned his arms. They covered his mouth with a handkerchief that smelled faintly of his mother's perfume. The scent brought back an Easter from his childhood: pink candy-covered almonds on a festive tablecloth—then nothing. He woke up in the morning feeling tired but with no recollection of what had occurred. At work, he was overcome by a strange need to call his mother, which he did, during his lunch break. Her voice was soothing and he blamed himself for not calling her more often after her stroke. On March 5, 2015, Hugo woke up a little before 2 am with an urgent need to pee. He took two steps out into the hallway where he saw three small creatures in surgical masks and lab coats, each no more than two feet tall, engaged in a strange preparation outside his son's bedroom. Hugo was alarmed because he had never before seen creatures of this sort. He managed to take one step toward them, an attempt to protect his boy, but the creatures were much stronger than their size would suggest. They easily wrestled him facedown to the floor, pinned him by his arms. They covered his mouth with a handkerchief that smelled faintly of his mother's perfume, a scent from childhood that had returned to him a little over two years ago without apparent cause or reason. The scent guided him to a memory of one of his mother's outfits from one of their first Christmases in the States, a green dress with shoulder pads and gold buttons down the front. Then blackness. He woke up in the morning feeling tired but with no recollection of what had occurred. At work, he was overcome by a strange need to call his mother, which he did, during his lunch break. At the clinic where she was recovering from another stroke, the third in a matter of three years, he left a message with the nurse who assured him she would pass on the message to his mother because the frail woman would find comfort in hearing that her son had thought of her. He blamed himself for not visiting his mother more often. On January 3, 2018, Hugo woke up from a strange dream around 1:30 am. In the dream, three small creatures in surgical masks and lab coats, each no more than two feet tall, had entered the house in the middle of the night and were in his son's bedroom inspecting the stuffed animals in the boy's toy basket. Hugo managed to grab one of the small creatures by the back of the neck but the creatures were stronger than their size would suggest and they quickly subdued him. They pinned him to the floor and covered his mouth with a fragrant handkerchief. In a dream, he woke up the next morning without any memory of what had occurred and later called his mother from work. In bed, now wide awake and hopeful for cover in darkness, Hugo was so terrified of the dream and of the image of those creatures and of the idea of having his memory erased that he found himself unable to move from under the covers. He remained very still, afraid to make any kind of sound that would betray him. He stayed like that for hours. He stayed like that even when he started to hear a faint shuffling on the hardwood floor in the hallway. The sound was like that of three sets of little feet shuffling back and forth outside his son's bedroom, but Hugo could not bring himself to go look.

GHOST

I'm rummaging through the dresser, tossing clothes that still smell like Sammy. I don't know what I'm looking for. But I'm committed so I open and toss and open and toss and the repetition is enough. To focus. To stop picturing her slumped against that tree. Alone. My Sammy. I hear Zay in the other room going on about how we need to ghost before they come for the rest of us. Who's they, I should ask. But I don't need to.

I find what I didn't know I was looking for and I'm back to myself. Cold in my hand, denser than I expected. I stash it in my bag, kick over the dresser. Kick the wall. Twice, four times. I'm counting, too, because my mind is racing. Zay finds me in Sammy's room and says, No time for this. There's a look in his eye that I don't understand. It's not panic. Let's go, he says.

In the kitchen, Tow and Rez are stuffing printers and scanners into duffle bags. All the equipment goes. Furniture stays. This is the Plan B we prepared to never use.

Sammy used to say: Nize, if something happens one day, you ghost. You do that for me. Philly, Chicago, doesn't matter where. Just ghost, for real. Promise me.

She put the palm of her hand on my chest when she talked like that. Raised it slow like a morning, like she wanted me to full stop. She did, too. Make me. Stop.

Nothing's happening, I said, so many times I did, because I wanted to be the one to make everything ok.

And now something is happening. Happened. I watch Tory grabbing what she can out the pantry. Zay comes back from the hall and throws me a clean shirt. He says, Lay low for a few hours and whatever you do, don't roll together. The one I'm wearing is soaked. I'll call you once I get the cash from the safe house, he adds.

Was it Wraith? I ask though I know, because I don't want to not ask.

Zay says no. No, again. He grabs me by the shoulders, says, Keep it together, alright. I'll get you Sammy's cut, too, he also says.

— // — // —

I knew Zay, and Zay knew Rez and Rez knew Tow. It was Zay that put us on. He was the plug, really. Got the first scanner when his uncle went away. That was the start.

First year or so, just me and Zay in a coupe. Didn't know anything back then — hit up malls with no disguise or anything. Just our faces on the closed circuit security feeds. It was small time, though. We got jeans and coats, mostly. Couple hundred a piece each hit. A little jewelry every now and again. Didn't think of much beyond each get, just came back on the block with some fresh gear and gifts for whatever girls we were trying to smash. They'd ask where we got shit like that and we told them not to worry. Said: Baby girl, chill, there's plenty more where that came from.

When Rez came on, he recruited our first source. She cost us half a dime but we got like twenty cards off her. We did numbers that put some real paper in our pockets for the first time, and Rez got dap for that. He was humble about it, though. Other guys with a scheme like that might go solo. But Rez was one of us and we were all-in. Together. Next was more sources: department stores, supermarkets, electronics stores. We never hit the same spot twice. Get and go and skate on them, be out. And don't fall in love with the merch. It's a means, that's all. That was our philosophy, anyway. Skated on them after each get. Some cards we sold, some cards we used. And on and on and on.

Sammy came later. She dropped in with Tow one day. White heels, sunglasses indoors — all kinds of extra. At first I thought they were together but Tow said to me: Not girlfriend, actress. Like he knew what I was thinking. Sammy sat on the beige leather love seat, across from Zay and Rez who sat on the big couch. She answered all their questions while I watched from the side with Tow. It was a job interview. Professional, like at a bank or something. Sammy didn't look at me during the whole thing. Not once. They asked her to do accents and she matched different expressions to each one. We couldn't believe it. She was from another world.

Zay said: Well, I think we found our face.

Rez: Yup, she sharp.

$$— // — // —$$

Sammy was core to us. Other faces came later: Reyna, Dame, Zee. They were hooks, though. Add-ons, not really the type that carried jobs on their own. Tory came last but she came as Rez's girl so she was core in a different type of way. And she was good, too. But Sammy was different. She just knew how to hold people's attention. She could convince any *one* of any *thing*, so she recruited and trained the others when they came on. She taught them what to say, how to hold eye contact. Shit from psych books. At a site, when it was time to rake, Sammy knew which employee to target, what clothes to try on. She saw the whole con from the start. Used pauses like opportunities. Took courage just to talk to her. First time I told her my name she just looked at me. Said: I know.

First time I got paired with her she already had a rep. This was months later and she'd been raking every job. We were at a department store and she was paying for about three stacks worth of gear but the clone wasn't working. She was face, I was the eyes. The girl at the register tried the card again and now there was another customer in line. We didn't like witnesses. Nothing good about more eyes on us. The girl at the register said: No, still not working. Another customer jumped in line. I saw Sammy pretend to look in her wallet for another card, stalling, and a manager came up to the girl at the register and asked, Is everything ok here? The card is declined, the girl said to the manager and the manager told her, Just call it in. More customers. There was a line now. I moved in with the distraction. Plan B. No biggie, get everyone out. But just as I got there Sammy looked up from her wallet with the fake ID in her hand and asked the girl and the manager, Can't I just open up a store card? The girl said: Yes, and the manager said: Of course, and now I was there, ready with the script of what to say playing in my head except Sammy had already cleaned up. And it was so obvious, her solution. I stopped trying to think of what to do and some of the people in line looked at me. But Sammy put her hand to my chest. First time she did that. So calm, too. I swear she could have stopped a hurricane right then, there. She said: Hi, honey, did you find those jeans? Cleanest two-comma accent you ever heard. And everyone in line believed we were a couple. I believed it, too. Girl at the register said: Congratulations, you've been approved.

Sammy got the card, a new fake account, and we walked around the store together. Now I was a face, too. Sammy said I might as well try on some clothes and she waited for me while I went in the changing room. I came out in some dress pants and a shirt. She said I looked handsome. I'd never been called that word before.

I was putting my clothes back on when she walked through the curtain and started kissing me. That was our first time. We walked out of that store with all the gear and a new card, too. That was the start of new things. Up until then we'd been making clones. We hadn't thought of opening accounts. Sammy changed that on the spot.

From then on, I got protective. Worried about her on every job. The way she looked at me was a redemption. At some point, I told her I wanted out. I told her we had some money put away and that was enough to start fresh, somewhere else. To have a normal life, I said. She laughed. That sounds awful, she said. Kissed me.

Jobs got easier but only because we got better at the work. Wavy, though. Bags. Every job was bags. That's when we started selling IDs, too. It was smaller than it could have been, just enough to get enough but never enough to attract attention. That was the approach I wanted. Careful. I fought for that, too. Argued with Rez and Zay and they agreed. Eventually. Tory, too. Tow was a mountain of calm, always steady on everything. Said: What's good's good. And that was it. All of us were one movement. We voted and made decisions together, agreed on targets and objectives. It was a business but it was family, too, for the six of us. Thanksgivings and Christmases, parties and vacations — Zay would pay and call it a company expense. Sometimes I wondered where all the money came from. We were good but the work wasn't easy. And Wraith was around by then, but back at that time he was more into that putting hot cars in containers business. So we kept doing our thing but watching. Careful. Wraith was kind of there but not there, and I worried but nobody else seemed to. Just one of those things.

One time, down in Miami, Zay bounced a burned clone. We were at a club and there had been bottles and more bottles and Zay must have lost track of what he was doing. He reached for the check, like always. Then the waitress came back and said: This card was reported stolen. Zay looked up from his glass and his eyes were miles away. He smiled at the girl like he hadn't heard what she said and he put his arm round her waist like he was about to kick it to her. Me and Sammy heard and she got up from my lap. I'm sorry, she said, to stall, but the waitress just handed the card back to Zay and said to Sammy: Look, I need to get paid tonight, so do you have another card or nah?

There were situations like that every now and then. Half the hustle was reacting quickly and Sammy was the best at that. She knew what to say; knew when to say nothing, too. She saw deeper in people and she adjusted to fit each situation. I felt like I'd won some lottery because I couldn't understand why she was with me.

— // — // —

First time Sammy mentioned ghosting, we were in bed with the lights on. She was scrolling through her phone. I was making notes about some site I'd scouted. This was early on.

She asked me, What would you do if something happened to me?

I didn't understand: Something happened?

Yeh. If I got caught, or something.

I'd come get you.

I'm serious, Nize.

Me too.

She was silent for a minute, then she asked if I believed in heaven and I said no. I laughed, too. She was serious, though. Asked if I believed in hell and I said yes. She said that didn't make sense: You can't believe in one and not the other.

I told her I'd seen hell. I know *that*, I said. I might have still been writing notes. Probably didn't even look up from the paper. When she grilled me some more I flipped it on her, asked if she believed in heaven.

Of course, she said. Then she got quiet for a bit so I put the notebook down. I tried to think of what to say but nothing came. She said: That's the saddest shit you ever said to me.

There was broken disappointment in her eyes.

I asked, Why, because I didn't really know any words that I could say to fix the way she was looking at me.

Because then we'll never see each other again, she said.

I shrugged.

So you think we just go in the dirt and that's it?

That's how it's been for everybody I known.

I pull up on low to Wraith's block. Some heads on a stoop but I'm at enough distance where they don't see me. That's got to be where Wraith stays. I let the engine run and watch. A couple of cars roll past, no biggie. I'm watching, waiting, but I keep seeing Sammy slumped against that tree. How she didn't look back at me, didn't respond when I held her. Her blood on my shirt.

I'm thinking of times in bed with her and it's like those moments are still happening, and also like they're about to happen for the first time again. I close my eyes and it's like time isn't real and she's not dead. Keep them closed for a second. When I open them, a grandmother is walking by with a grocery bag in one hand, a small black purse at her ribs. She notices me but she knows better than to look. In the side-view mirror, she disappears and then she's the one who's not real. Maybe.

I have two missed calls and a text from Mom, which is how I have Zay saved in my phone. The text says: *miss you*

I hit the green phone button and Zay goes, Where you at?

I'm ghost.

Good. You talk to the others?

Nah.

Ok. Listen, Tow and Rez already got their shares. You're last. You ready to meet?

Yeh.

Alright. The crib on Waydell. Twenty minutes.

I see you there.

When me and Zay got to Sammy she was around on the other side of the tree. Couldn't see her from the parking lot. When I saw her, the first thing I noticed was that her shoes were gone. Her head limp to the side like life deflated out of her. At first I thought she was pretending. Like it could be a joke. But I knew. Even before I knew, I knew.

— // — // —

One time at the outlets upstate, Sammy got questioned by security because they thought she was shoplifting. They had police there and everything. That was the closest we ever came to getting caught on the job. She had fake IDs on her, multiple identities for the day's run. If they looked through her wallet they'd find everything. She'd be done.

Tow was her eyes that day. I was working with Tory, at another store in the same outlet. When Tow put out the code red, I rushed to the site. Not smart but Sammy needed me. I didn't think. Or maybe I did.

Security questioned her for a good twenty minutes, about as long as it took us to get down there. I hovered as if there was anything I could do. Police told her they'd received an anonymous tip about a ring working the area. I was convinced Wraith had tipped them off but Zay and Rez said it couldn't be. Either way, Sammy was a pro. Played her part. Gave up nothing. I imagined her saying something like: How dare you question me, do you know how much money I spend at your stores? Or something like that. It was only later that she told me how it had really gone down. She had pulled receipts of stuff she'd raked at other stores: some of the day's haul that she carried with her as part of the con. And they believed her, backed off and apologized. She always said that walking in with shopping bags was the best way to make the salespeople think she was about to buy something at their store.

She didn't say anything on the drive back but when we got back to our place I hugged her so hard her shoulder cracked. I'm ok, she said, because she believed she was. This is the business we in, she said.

Later that night, after we'd turned off the lights, she hugged me in bed and said, I was so afraid I wouldn't see you again. If I'd gone to jail, what would you have done? Would you ghost?

— // — // —

I call Tow but he doesn't answer. Rez, too. They're already ghost, but probably not like me. I reach in my bag. Hold the piece for a bit before I pull it out. It looks like it looked when I found it in the dresser but not like I remember it looking before that. Still ready, though, like metal always is. Sammy hated this thing.

When I was six, my mother got sick of being both mom and dad, so she ghost. A few years later, the people who took me in gave me their last name. They thought it would be easier on me to go through life that way. We want you to be part of this family, my new mother said, but she couldn't be my mother. I felt sorry for her that she didn't understand that. I was young, but not as young as her.

Wraith walks out of the house with the busy stoop. There's a goon trailing behind, hoody over his head. Wraith is popping shit with the kids on the stoop but it's just jokes. He acts like nothing is wrong or right, just is. Maybe it wasn't Wraith who pulled the trigger on Sammy. Maybe it was someone else. I don't really know. What I do know is Sammy is missing from me. On my chest there's the ghost of the palm of her hand and there is no home for me anymore. I check my mirrors again. All cars, parked; no witnesses. Wraith says something to the heads and they scatter, disappear around the corner. He gets into a car with the goon. Passenger side.

I picture the face of the woman who wasn't my mother. She thought that by giving me a new name she could make me a different person, that I could become someone else. Her son. Maybe she really believed that shit. Maybe she hoped I'd believe it. Maybe she was doing it for me, maybe for herself. It was a lesson, though, that new name. All around me, I started to understand people for what they are — one thing trying to pass itself off as another. Once I learned that, the world made sense.

Wraith's car pulls out. I roll down my window. A ghost. They're rolling in my direction. This is the end but they don't know it. I stay low, hide behind the glare. They're talking in the car, and their faces come into focus. But it's not Wraith and a goon. It's Wraith and Zay, watching their mirrors for danger on their tail. And then it's not just me seeing them because they see me right back. They look surprised once they see me aiming the barrel. And then their car is stopping and they're reaching for something. The story is always the same. We all know to be careful but we watch for the wrong thing. Already dead but don't know it yet. Ghosts like everybody we known.

THE DEAD

The beginning is not what happens first. Is what comes before. I saw her before she was mine like a whisper is a feather is a bird is an egg is a bird. She was mine before she was. So let's not think of beginnings through the lens of sequence. Let us consider, instead, that every cause is an effect is a cause is a breath on the skin of another. And so I propose the following: for understanding a beginning, the middle is better. She found me on Elm Street, at Saint James, but she could just as well have found me at Saint Michael's. Across town. Is it out of hope or despair that we name our hospitals after saints? It is a thing worth knowing. A distinct line divides one from the other, hope from despair, that is similar to the line that divided my flesh from hers. If not at first. At first, her flesh was my flesh. More, even. She was no different from me than my arm is different from my leg ear knee breast. She was mine in the way that I am mine, then she was more removed though mine still, then an entity separate entire. Together we had breakfast on Ferry, first at one bakery then moving the weekly ritual to a newer place. Years like seconds had converted from not yet being to having already been. We watched the shoppers. The families and the loners with their bags and newspapers while we sipped galões, that most Portuguese named of coffees. Sometimes we bought sardines, even before she liked them. This middle, as described here, is a much better way of arriving at the beginning because even before it arrived I had dreamed it. I had said, as others do, "One day I will warn her about boyfriends and what they really mean when they say they want you." But the ending came unannounced. Now the beginning again: she was my song; the best me was when I was with her. Though I was less than my best, too, with her. But that is to say not very much at all. So this: I can describe all of my meaning with just one sentence — parents are not meant to bury their children. One sentence is everything and yet not nearly enough. One sentence does not convey the crevasse of nothing stretching in all the directions. One sentence is a surrender, a coward's way of narrating a life. Instead I hold on to the little I have of her, which is quite a lot except in comparison with all there is to remember. For instance, how many times did she wear this yellow sweater with her black jeans? So many gaps to fill. I imagined my existence would be like so many. I waited for the beginning, which was my daughter, and then what followed the beginning of her being born. I don't have to learn all the languages to know they are all inadequate because no language has perfected the word for emptiness. Or this: what's the word for the promise of a memory of something that will never come to pass? Let the languages conspire to describe that one, what is it to me? No word, no sentence, just the absence of her from the world. Her end came before mine and what sense is there to make of that? What order can we apply when even this empty room is a reminder? The nothing includes me, as it must include so much else that escapes my sight. I cannot confirm. So now this, which is all that remains: the ending is not what happens last. What happens last comes earlier, if there is a witness to account. Otherwise, the ending comes before, more like the middle, which is also where the beginning lies. It's not so different at all. Sequence is a betrayal. Order is a fiction.

Avô

His flawless routine. The tea pot whistle: the slow pour: the towel draped over his head: his face over the bowl: the steam emanating. A home-remedy to soothe the pain. At some point in the night, me alone in my bed, his screaming started. Ai. Ai. Ai. Ai. Ai. Pause. Silence. The dark. Ai. I startled and the small of my nine-year-old back felt cold. Ai. I wondered if the neighbors could hear him. Embarrassed. Ai. Ai. Ai. I remembered his tales at the athletic club in downtown Lisbon where we went to shower before we had our own tub at home. Past the Greco-Roman wrestlers grappling on mats, beyond a boxing ring I was too small to peer over, posters of champions past and present. He'd point to the wall at the faded papers with the crumpled corners. *Neno won the title in '41. I was his sparring partner.* Another one, *In '32 I beat Amadeu. He was champion in '36.* A life in memories he'd forgotten, mostly, except for the highlights. After so many years the remembering was hard. He searched for dates. Backtracked, corrected himself. We walked through and familiar faces said hello. He shook hands, his shoulders slumped. They didn't know his pain. At night again. Whistle: pour: towel: bowl: steam. Then later the screams returned, echoes of punishment his face had absorbed from men who didn't remember his name. *I almost had a shot in '38. Eduardo broke his hand and a replacement was needed.* Pause. His mind shuffling through the memories. *Money changed hands. They gave someone else the fight.* All these years later I don't know what hurt him more — never getting a shot or the nightly burning that stabbed at his face. From him I learned that the punch doesn't always hurt in the moment. Ai. Ai. Ai. Ai. I waited for the screaming to start again. Ai. Ai. I knew his hands were over his face. My grandmother in bed next to him all those years. Her devotion not enough to heal him. Ai. Ai. Ai. A few summers later, when I returned home for a family visit, my uncle drove on a highway outside Lisbon, pointed right and up at a hillside cemetery in the distance. *Your grandfather is buried there.*

DIARY

October 7
Dear, Diary

I promise keep you safe make sure you not found cant tell you how much more now theyre are percautions to be very careful you are my Diary and I am yours as well I am so happy to meet you too more soon ok bye.

Sincerely,
Roxie

— // — // —

October 10
Dear, Diary

Its three days when I write but ok I hope you not mad miss you the hole time to want to write everyday so I can tell all the things I still got you hiding under the counter behind the big pot also I got a fake Diary fake hidden by my bed where Joc can find it I write in their some times so he think he know long as he think he know he dont look for nothing thats pretty smart you ask me.

Every thing else is same Joc keep coming and going Joc say he got big moves coming been changed his shcedule as well going out during the day to yesterday he going on and on you know some thing about being close he always talk like that saying not saying then later he tell me he tell me already some thing he think he tell but only thougth but not said you know.

Ok I dont push my luck now try to write again tommorow but if I cant then tommorow well defenitely next day I miss you when I dont write you stay safe.

Yours,
Roxie

— // — // —

October 12
Dear, Diary

Sorry I not write yesterday here I am thow Joc was home all day I get not one moment alone I hope you forgive me sorry honest.

Things are good but Joc is very pairanoide now at first I thougth ok it was from him finding other Diary before he was very mad once that happened but then that past and now its being three weeks so I think he freaked out on some thing else his shcedule still all over the place he come home and go all crazy times too he tell me eat alone if hes is not back last night I even not feel him get into the bed till the sun already coming up then two hours later he gone again and now its five hes out one more time I find out whats going on I hope soon.

I did get to go out yesterday Joc took me the super market I pick fresh veggies some frozen ones too thow for us that made me so happy also I saw Anthony who you dont know really but hes a boy I used to go to school with way back when first Im not think Anthony reconize me cause he look at us but then look away he just keep moping the floor like he been doing but then when we by the frozen foods I catch Anthony staring one more time so I think he know me once he see me see him he run off gone I not see him then.

The super market was so much fun too I love all the color-ful fruits veggies as well I walk up and down that isle a good three times till Joc start yelling me to hurry on up I just let my hand go right accross the top feel the different skins I pic-ture the dirt where they grow I never seen a farm not once in real life any way thow I did see pictures and in movies thats not like really being on farms in real life must smell so good so big maybe one day Joc and me watch we can actualy pick fruits from some trees I think the farmers would let us if we ask nice but I cant ask Joc for that now cause all that man see is something else say the people who got my mom close to done but ok I hardly even remember her its been so long so just give me piece of mind already but Joc at this for years so it might be nice to have it done with after all these time instead him just going on and on about it.

Thats all thats happen I cant write tommorow cause its Sunday and Joc be home all day long on Monday tell you every thing I dont you worry you just stay hidden Joc dont find you either ok and I take care the rest ok.

Love,
Roxie

— // — // —

October 15
Dear, Diary

Sorry I know not write I swear these have been the two worse days of my life Joc come home hurt night before last I not even knowing what to do blood and his face pretty bad as well I give him ice bath help him too cause he not even moving without pain he say it was so long to get his clothes off he screaming the hole time help him in the tub he keep grab his ribs saying he hurt just to breath man he crying then he cant sleep even cause he keep crying and crying pain I think he got broken ribs or some thing then he taking quick breaths all night long this man who can going to sleep like that not me I tell you.

I dont know what to do no more so tired he cant sleep cause the pain Im up to with him I try read him a story like he done for me when I was little I dont know nothing else make him feel better but he say no dont want me read tell me to leave him the fuck alone which ok fine use that language with me and see where you get all I try to do was help so I say fine you can take care of your own self good luck now bye ok.

I got to go back to the room now cant be away too long he might wake up I just want to write dont worry Im fine I worry about Joc he a real pain in my butt he really try to catch bad guys and now hes is gone and got hurt but Im trying help him get better you watch and dont you worry I keep writing too I write much as I can even if its hard while hes home he will be home for awhile as well in a lot of pain ok good bye now.

Sincerely,
Roxie

— // — // —

October 17
Dear, Diary

Sorry I not write yesterday Joc got worst and worst the pain to much for him he scream all night long and I got worry some neighbor go call the cops we not sleep not even one minute either in the morning he give me a number to call and thats when I know is a serious business cause I never use the phone only Joc any way the number is Teresas shes is his mom I tell her what happen on the phone that Joc hurt she could come by bring some medacine or something I think shes a nurse.

Shes is so wierd soon as she walk in she ask why we leave the curtains close during the day I tell her hello is she blind people can look in from out side a home is private not for every body she say fine with a face Im like is not for you to like I take her to our room and she not even caring about Joc just start to get really confused ask where I sleep at I tell her on the bed where else people sleep thow she say no what about my bed point to me so I say again right their and with some atittude too if she judging my house ok Joc taking short breaths I feel crazy out of my mind I did not get no sleep neither but Teresa not even getting why shes there making a face at me I say oh but then Joc scream tell me leave so she could give him medacine I just close the door harder then I had to too.

They talk in theyre for a minute I think the medacine work cause Joc finaly sleep last night good thing too cause then I sleep some as well but any way I hear Teresa talk to Joc in their way they got loud a few times ok but then Joc tell her to shhhh and she did talk lower it must of been some good medacine too he not crying no more after that.

When she come out the room she ask I remember her like what is she thinking with her strange questions I say of course she ask if I know who she is she must think Im stupid I dont really know I tell her I know who she is very well cause she is Jocs mom thank you now what game she playing she must want to be confusing with me she ask again the same thing too and I make a face like no other questions also I dont understand her neither she strange woman used to be in a crazy house I know that for years too Joc say not to be paying her no attention to what she say cause she nothing but a crazy woman but Joc desparate and in all that pain too their was no one else can help Joc me too need sleep you know I even ask him if he want go to the hospital he say no no absolutely no not ok.

Well Teresa went before that she talk about I got to sleep on the couch or find nother bed like excuse me that I cannot sleep there with Joc and very wierd but I keep looking at the bedroom door closed Teresa say Joc sleeping he need to rest so I just stay on the couch once she gone then things went back to normal kind of me and Joc got some sleep finaly and good thing too cause this morning he still sleep so I got some time to write tell you every thing thats happen I did miss you so much as things happening I keep thinking I got to remember all the important parts so I can tell you every thing too Im so happy I remember it all just like it happen I think ok now I push my luck I go check on Joc but I write again soon as I can to will think of you all the time till then I hope you miss me when I not writing you know.

All my love,
Roxie

— // — // —

October 20
Dear, Diary

I really miss you these last few days being home with Joc all day long hard as well he so needy want me stay in the bed room with him all day long too I cant even do a very normal work out or some thing in the living room without him calling from the bed just ask what Im doing or get water I not tell him about Teresa either he ask me massage his feet or legs talk about he bed sore please its not stop his ribs better thow he still in the bed I mean he still need the meds but at least we both can sleep now good thing too.

He really very annoying about this like a baby or some thing this man complaint about every thing so needy yesterday he getting so bad on my last nerve I tell him I cant find no more medacine now I know I got to give it to him at some point come later on but it so much fun watch him a little get worry that we had lost the med or throwed them out in the garbage or some thing that man cursing up a storm too he almost got up out of the bed as well he so worry and I had a good laugh just by myself in the bathroom with the water running like washing up or some thing he not know neither.

Another thing that still happening is I keep thinking about Teresa all the time what she say to me about remembering her she ask it in such a strange way too I know full well she know I know her cause I seen her before many times even dont try to be funny the whole talk so strange I cant talk to Joc or tell him any thing cause well first of all he sick enough as is and also annoying as well I dont even want to start that kind of thing with him now but also cause he just yell at me for cooking things up in my own head all the time well women just know these things some times theyre is no good reason to be doing so he says thow I think too much all the time Diary you really the only one I can tell this to and these things theyre isnt even anything to talk about really just some thing on my mind.

I really wish I could see you that you could be a real actual live person you really easy talk to the only one I can talk too you make it so easy not judge neither I know you not real I know that just a diary but some times I really wish I can pull you out so we can be together talk really talk so I can hear your voice and you hear mine as well.

I write again soon as I can.

Much love,
Roxie

— // — // —

October 22
Dear, Diary

I got to write fast Joc probaly wake up any minute but I just got to tell you something that happen so strange today.

So ok we low on food and Joc really want some steak I tell him I got some pork I can make hes not trying to hear that on and on about the steak so I finaly say if he want steak I run to the store get some but none here sorry so I said that likes some thing to end it cause Joc always want to be the one do the shopping I only go with him some times I dont even like leaving the apartment no more really now in days men eyes always on me but oh well Joc want the steak so bad that he actualy say yes which is news to me I could go get steak at the store and quick too not happy either but I go just the same hes such a baby since he got hurt so agravating too.

But anyway I go to the store and guess who is there again but Anthony moping the floor by the meats like he not moved I see him soon as I turn that corner well not trying to get close but he see me alone walk right up to me ask if I was Roxie and I said yes of course thats my name dont wear it out cause Im trying to get this steak and go Anthony had the mop and bucket with him as well like some super hero cleaning to but he look real happy to see me like too happy I mean we used to be friends but that was a little wierd he say he not seen me so long since like seventh grade and I say I know he start talking about high school and where I go and I just tell him that I not going to school no more for a long time.

He just keep talking questions too I not really listening either then he say something to me he say I look older like a lady I just laugh at this boy said bye that was funny you know like I am a woman I have a home relationship and Joc really need me right now cause he sick I tell Anthony all that too and he fell back some any way it was really wierd conversation and I rush home and it feel like something behind me the whole time but every time I turn around nothing there but air.

But anyway I come home make the steak Joc so happy boy this man simple we had a good night together too watch a movie but then he fall asleep I just come write all this Anthony so wierd I tell you more tommorow when I get some more time dont miss me too much thow.

Love,
Roxie.

— // — // —

October 24
Dear, Diary

Sorry I not write yesterday I know I told you I write but what a crazy crazy day today was for me.

First Joc ask I have some new Diary so I got worry I play the game thow just say yes not one more word and he tell me he find it I was pretty sure he not found you but still not so sure he had the other one the fake Diary I was so happy when he tell me where he find it cause then I know its not you he got good thing too still he crazy about something else now not a reason to overeact. .

Also Joc say he feel better when for a walk so I though I clean bed room change sheets and wash them then I puting away summer clothes in the hall closet cause is cold now he wont wear those but till summer come again well theres a box their and its say DO NOT TOUCH just like that I left it but who is not going to see what thats about but honest I not mean to still it fell theirs tape all around its was a small shoe box I shook to make sure nothing broke any thing it sound like just papers and pictures maybe the whole apartment silent I hear nothing in the hallway or any thing I open the box take a quick look and ok some old pictures in there a young man and then I said this young Joc a woman and a baby as well some pictures also some letters also from a woman named Luisa too letters for Joc signed Luisa just like that Love, Luisa well I not understanding what they are about then I see my name clear as day on one of the letters I get excited you know look for more of my name cause why is there letters with my name from a woman I dont even know more letters with my name Roxie writen very clear many times I read a little bit of it but the handwriting so bad I cant make out even a word hardly.

Well then I hear the door close and I look up and Joc right theyre staring at me ask what I am doing with those letters cause they not mine he say and he ask if I read them I say no what is that box I ask him but he not saying not even one word he just turn and go right into bed room slam the door angry I get scared a little he look really mad when he seen me I start to think I got away with it but then he come to the kitchen when I am making dinner ask me again he say I should tell him the truth that I cant get in trouble if I just be honest I just keep stiring that pot no problem said no I nope hadnt even seen the box first cause I was just working on the clothes I said not till it fell he went back in the room and locked the door I heard him on the phone but when he came back out he not saying anything else about it just ate dinner real quiet then I cleaned up and we went to bed no movie or anything.

I though about those letters all night who is Luisa how does she know Joc how does she knows me Joc went out now took the box he said he be back in one hour and that time is almost up I better end this now I couldnt wait write again soon as I can.

Yours,
Roxie

— // — // —

October 25
Dear, Diary

Teresa come back today I open the door when the bell
ring and she come in very quiet not saying not one thing to
me and off straight to bed room shut the door she talked in
there with Joc for a long time he had told me she was coming.

I couldnt really hear what they talk about at first and I not
even try to honest the whole thing so crazy so I said no thank
you but why Teresa was there what they talk about did Teresa
know who is Luisa this even about Luisa.

Then all a sudden the door open and Teresa come out here
she was crying and she had the shoe box she touch my face
well nah I said moved back she ask again if I remember her
this time I just scream at her loud too you know I want to
know why she keep asking that stupid question too Joc come
out our room and I ask him why Teresa asking questions like
that I scream at him too but he not mad either or any thing
just standing their quiet like maybe he waiting on Teresa or
me too and he look tired a little weak then Teresa look at him
then she ask if I remember my mother and I start to say what
is this woman doing right now but Joc took the box and push
her out the door Teresa crying as well and she say something
about she need her own bed or something like that Joc tell
her be quiet call her a crazy woman ask if she feel like going
back to the crazy house he said he could make that happen
too and that she should be real careful as well round us then
Teresa the one look really weak like she about to just drop to
the floor she just kind of went along when Joc put her out I
was screaming at him thow what was going on and what she
meaned why she talking like that I keep saying but Joc not
saying not one word he threwords all the letters and pictures in

63

the sink every thing in that shoe box lit a match stood theyre just watch it burn I stand behind him but I could hear the paper cracking and every thing.

Well he went to bed not eating dinner or any thing I thougth about writing you all this but worry he could be still awake and you know good thing I not even think take you out cause when I got to the bed he was still awake crying all saying over and over if I know he love me and what not and I just say yeah but what thats got to do with I was confused cause theyre was a lot of things not making sense all a sudden thow he keep saying he love me so much and he not shutting up about it either so when he start touching me I let him do what he want to be done with it and get some sleep.

Sorry I drop all this on you but thats whats happen with me and its not fair to not tell you either you the only friend I have I have to be honest or else this hole thing means nothing its easy just to tell you things you just listen as well such a really good friend Diary.

The bestest love to you,
Roxie

— // — // —

October 28
Dear, Diary

Im sorry I not write is Joc been home a lot so a little hard to get space he finaly went out today saying hes is going back to work to get the people who hurt him say theyre the same people he after all these years that hes is really close to getting the people who got my mom thats why they hurt me he said I was like ok fine I dont care just do what you got to do already.

I look everywhere I can while he sleep and when he shower as well but theres nothing no boxes no pictures in this house I think that shoe box all the information I was ever going to get about who Luisa is but now its gone I thougth about going to Teresa ask her but I dont even know where she live I mean I know kind of but not really and she so crazy and I dont need Joc finding out that I did go and getting all mad at me Im just have to wait to really get anything about what this whole thing is maybe one day I find out but dont know thow whatever.

Im really sorry I pull you in this thing with all my writing to you here its just drama drama more drama thow you been so good too just listening I truley dont know how I would survived past these crazy weeks with out you the hard times I thougth about you and remember the important things so the story can make sense when I finaly write really you still are the best way better then all the other Diarys I had I wish their could be something I could do for you but maybe just trusting you like this is how I show you much I trust and what you really mean in my life a very special I have to go now more soon I promess.

All my love,
Roxie

— // — // —

October 30
Dear, Diary

So I guess this month not been weird enough so something else happen to really put it over the top I swear.

Joc is out right now wont be back till night time say hes back on the normal shcedule now going on and on about the guys hes is catching taking guns with him as well when he going out but whatever thats not the crazy part the real crazy part is that hes gone just now and the door bell ring not a big deal I just let it ring when Joc isnt home and whoever rings just thinks nobody is home they go away as well but then the bell keep ringing a second third forth fifth time come on now so I said to myself that if it ring just one more time I will go look it could be emergency I even thougth maybe is Luisa coming to me but I know crazy crazy I know thougth it cant be her but maybe if I not think about it would happen so the bell rang again six time so fine here I go walk down the stairs and look thru the peep hole and Anthony standing theyre from seventh grade and the store Anthony but he not with a mop or a bucket now I open the door and he standing their just like its ok I ask him how he know where I live and he said he saw Pudes on the doorbell easy but come on now I ask if he follow me home that one night I got the steak at the store and he said no but I could tell from his face it was yes he know very well he follow me to my house that night no way no doubt about that.

He said something like how he hadnt seen me at the store and he got worry and I told him that hes is only seen me twice thats nothing to start thinking about some body over but then he told me he love me said its a decalaration and I said to him that its really not a good idea to be talking like that cause I have someone in my life thank you and hes is upstairs to scare him off but he got all weird and said that he knew my dad went out and I was home alone but I just laugh and I say to him I am a woman and hes so stupid he dont even know thats not my father thats my boyfriend and we are very much in love thank you I told him too Anthony started saying wait and something else but I not even have time for all that I just close the door right on his face and said he better not ring my bell no more I think he get the message but you never know guys like that can be really dum thats why Joc not even want me going out too much.

Anyway thats weird and I hope Joc not find out that Anthony coming over here to talk cause then it might get real crazy ok thats all today I write tommorow with Joc back on shcedule it shouldnt not be so hard for me I talk to you soon bye.

Very much yours,
Roxie

$$— // — // —$$

October 31
Dear, Diary

Well so much for that Joc find out soon as he open the door yesterday already asking about who had come to the house I said no one we sat on the couch and he tell me its was very important cause he knew someone had been at the house how I let them in he mad too told me he had ways of knowing ways I cant imagine as well I should be honest also he said the way he knew was cause he had put a piece of tape on the door outside our apartment then came back the tape had moved so I not have no way other then the truth I say to him no one had been to the house but that I did had opened the front door cause Anthony come by and not quit ringing the bell well that meaned I had to explain who Anthony is and once I did that Joc shoot up like lightening about to go fix some things poor Anthony oh well he should learn thow I even thougth I should get you out to write all this but worry Joc might come right back so I wait played some music just wait.

I start to put away the laundry in the bed like I been doing

67

Joc had left his big coat on the bed ran out quick so I hang
it up on his side of the closet I never hang up his clothes he
always wants to do his own clothes but I dont like coats on
the bed its bad luck you know so I hang and theyre it was
under the black suit theirs a tiny dress not my dress and I
never seen it before but so beautiful so gorges I touch it smell
good too not like our house but like an old smell from some
where else I remember but cant remember.

First I hold it up in front of me to see in the mirror I look
again and it look like it could fit me all off my clothes I just
hold the dress in front of me again so pretty in the mirror I
thougth I know what Anthony meaned I do look like a woman I was a woman its was funny but I want to wear it on I
open the zipper and put the dress on I swear it fit like nothing I ever wore like just right for me too like some thing for
me weird so tell not one person I know its crazy to feel that
way about a dress I know not mine I imagine myself like in
a movie I see with Joc or something before I even born wearing the dress a party and Joc hold my hand and we in love as
well hard to see but I try anyway is hard think of something
you never seen you know but ok I do it I can feel how pretty
music keep playing cause I saw in the mirror pretty how I
look wear it like is just made for me just for me I spin around
too in it my head dizzy but ok I still fine music I spin again
dance as well and then one more time and it feel like I danc-
ing like I was some body else some body in some other life
just spining in front of a mirror and think that life can be like
as me oh well.

I hope this not too crazy I think it is but I think I can trust
you I write again soon I promess.

Forever yours,
Roxie

WISDOM

The rows of crops are avenues. The days succeeding like a shuffled deck in the deliberate hands of a dealer. The man speaks: *Kid, you got a girl?* The kid answers: *Of course.* Their wrists are strong. Their fingers are agile, sure under the bruising sun that browns and leathers their skin. *Let me guess,* the man says, *She waiting for you?* The kid answers, *Yeh, just two more years of this and I'll have enough to marry and buy a farm back home.* In the distance, a mule pushes a lonely complaint against the merciless walls of the afternoon air. *You're doing it right, kid,* the man says. *Yeh,* the kid adds, *I send her a little bit of money every month but I'm saving most of it.* Before him, dreams scaffold with abandon and there is no gravity to the years they encompass. *I have a girl back home, too,* the man says. *She's a woman now, actually. You'll see, after a while you won't write as often but keep sending money, that's the trick.* The kid grunts an acknowledgment but questions are already crowding his mouth. *How long have you worked here,* he asks. *Five, no, six years,* the man answers. *You been back,* the kid asks. *Yeah, but only once because you can't save that way,* the man says. The trip is expensive and dangerous, and the job doesn't wait so to return home is to lose the small steps that have already been taken and to leave again is to restart from scratch. The man doesn't say this but he says it. *And she's waiting for you to marry,* the kid asks. *Of course,* the man answers, pulling his eyes away from the work and looking up at the kid, a confusion bordering on nausea over-taking him. He grimaces, puts a hand to his forehead: *I think I stood too quickly.* He glances out at the work yet to complete, the rows like a promise curling away from him into the distance of the earth's curvature, then he looks back at the small neat patch they have completed only to turn his eyes from it again, its smallness too much. In the distance, the rows remain. They're longer now, stretching beyond the places his eyes can reach. The kid follows the man's gaze off into the horizon. The kid doesn't look back yet, doesn't know to. They bend at the waist again, their joints aching of a nameless thirst. *Kid, you're doing it right,* the man says and the kid draws a breath to last a lifetime. *Of course.*

THE AMBIT OF YOUR
ON-COURT PERSONA

I remember the time Ray dunked on me. It was a Tuesday. We were running half-court looks in practice. The player I was defending used a baseline pick, flashed out to the three-point line. The ball behind me on the opposite wing, I didn't chase all the way. I played the odds, aware it would take a perfect pass to beat me, and blocked the man setting the pick on me to keep him from cutting to the basket. I kept one eye on the ball and saw it float into the post. Lane cleared and Ray had his man sealed, no one between him and the hoop, and the lob was immaculate. All I remember is racing over there. My goal: be a human obstacle. Well, Ray didn't care that I was in the way. I might as well not have been there — that's how much difference I made. He took off, I mean launched, and cleared me by half a foot. Way over my head. I just stood there.

His dunk, the sound of it behind and above me, I'm not exaggerating: I thought he broke the backboard. I think I had my eyes closed. I stumble-ran-fell out of the way and when I looked back, the players on the court, on both offense and defense, were laughing at me. All of them, just laughing. And one of them, I don't remember who, but one of them said: "Hey JV, don't get in Ray's way. You get hurt like that." So I know it wasn't Ray, but somebody there said it. And I just picked up the basketball and tried to get the game going again as quickly as I could.

— // — // —

Game day flow: we have an away game and the bus will be leaving in the next twenty or so. I'm in the lobby polishing off an Italian Hot Dog from Leo's. I'm devouring this thing; the potatoes and the ketchup, and Leo drizzles the hot sauce in layers. A dime. I'm with Larry and Marcus. They each have their own dog, too. We're yelling at each other because

Coach has just finished going over the spreadsheets with all the info on our opponents. Larry is telling Marcus that just because this team has low rebounds it doesn't necessarily mean they're bad rebounders. Or worse, small. He tells Marcus to look at the field-goal percentage, says that because they don't miss as many shots there are less boards to snag. Ray drifts over to us, sits opposite me listening to the banter.

Larry is making a good point but *I'm* the point guard. Even as a transfer who's only been at this school for a few months, it's *my* job to make good points. I chew as quickly as I can and chime in. I pull out my copy of the spreadsheet, point out the turnovers and convince them that we should pressure the ball on defense.

Crowd them, I say. They nod. I add: *That's* the game-plan.

I glance at Ray and he, too, looks convinced. It's easy to persuade people: find an aspect they haven't considered and deliver your words succinctly and with authority.

As I'm walking to the bus I see Ray talking to Coach in the vestibule. My eyes catch Ray's and he stops mid-sentence. Coach doesn't look happy. I don't know what to make of it. Everything is still new at this school.

— // — // —

On the bus, I turn to Marcus in the seats across the aisle. His headphones are a quarantine so I gesture with my hands, ask him to lean in. He slides away his red Roshes with the white soles, obliges. I ask if he's talked to Ray.

Like, today? he asks.

Today, yesterday, this week. Have you even heard his voice?

I think so, he says. Seems distracted, repeats: I think so.

Don't you think he's acting weird?

Not really. Then, after a pause: Looks normal to me.

You'd make an awful point guard.

Maybe he's stressing. He's a senior.

So, and I'm a junior transfer.

Yeah, but senior year is all about where you're going to play next year. People stress over shit like that.

I know it's stressful, that's not what I'm saying. What I'm asking is if he's looked different to you.

Maybe things ain't going so well with him and Tonya, you know what I'm saying?

Really? Tonya's Ms. Perfect Everything.

I don't know but I heard he's after Sharon now. They're together all the time.

Really?

Yup.

No more Tonya for Ray?

Marcus smiles, proud of the connection he has just made. Says: Something's rotten in the country of Denland.

What?

It's from a book.

I think that's Denmark.

Nope, *Hamlet*.

I shake him off: I saw Ray talking to Coach before we got on the bus and it looked heated. I think something's up.

Marcus shrugs, headphones go back in. As he reclines, I see the bottom of his shoes and notice a brown spot polluting one of his otherwise virgin-white soles.

— // — // —

Thing about Ray: he was so fundamentally sound. His dribbling: never off-balance. His feet steady as pillars under his weight. His jump-shot was an artist's rendering. A symmetry of angles, from his right elbow to the alignment of his hips to the direction of his shoulders. Precise, is what he was.

Standing behind him in the layup line, you could catch yourself watching him because everything he did seemed so proper. He was never rushing but always getting to his spot on time. And there were times early that season when he caught me watching him and asked me what I was doing. But I was trying to learn, so that I could do what he did in the same way he did it.

A few weeks into the season, something shifted in me. For the first time in my life, I wanted to lead though I didn't know exactly what that might mean. So I just did it. A new school was a shot at a new identity. I started slowly. I made sure I was the first in line for warm up drills; I became the one to set the pace in practice, had others follow *me*. That way, I figured, I wouldn't be following Ray. At that point, I was motivated by a joke Larry and Marcus had made, calling me Mini-Ray. For two months now they had joked about my name, about JV not being a varsity name, so it wasn't the teasing that bothered me. Something else got to me about it. They thought they were being funny when they called me Mini-Ray but it was a silly accusation, really, because everyone wanted to be like Ray. He was the leading scorer and a good student, too, very sharp. He was so big he covered the sun. Not tall, either. I mean, he was tall, but that's not what I mean. He was big, sure, but his presence was huge. So when he caught me staring at him, as he had a few times, I'd ask for the ball and pretend that I was just waiting my turn. He'd pass the ball but sometimes he'd stare at me after the fact as if he were seeing in me something he hadn't been expecting to see. I imagine it was the same look he'd have given if he had turned with the ball in his hands to find a Martian eagerly waiting for a pass.

I desperately wanted to be my own person but I was uneasy about becoming a leader. I conceived of it as a role, and Ray was still the captain whereas I had never led anything.

On the court was easier; in the flow of the game or the drills, I had no time to think. Still, the locker room posed challenges. During home games my tactic was easy enough but for away games, in situations where each locker room presented a different layout, I never knew where I should change. I was very self-conscious. I took to hanging near the back of the line so that once I walked into the locker room I could spot where Ray was changing and park my stuff at a distant corner. That did the trick for a while but then one time I walked into the locker room and there was nowhere to change except right next to Ray. I tried to avoid looking at him but trying to do so was sort of like trying to hold in a sneeze while staring directly into a light. I must have signaled my discomfort because Ray asked me if I was ok and I couldn't even speak. I just nodded and he kept staring at me, like confused.

From then on I made it a point of being first to the locker room, which had the added benefit of being something a leader might do. It also allowed me to avoid the Mini-Ray accusation. But then, invariably, I'd arrive at the urinal for a preemptive strike to find Ray working on the same bladder schedule. So I'd fall back and pretend to wash my hands only to have him appear like a revelation at the sink next to me. Hiding in a stall didn't work. I had to pull down my shorts and sit to piss, which was a different sort of uncomfortable. And then we'd get on the court and Ray would look like he was floating on air and jumping without effort. And then we'd be back in the locker room and I'd have to avoid and hide. Or worse, pretend.

— // — // —

Season is in full swing now. We practice just about every day, except for days when we have games. Ray is the star of the team but I'm grooving. My game is thriving. My assists are up, my turnovers down. My defense is solid, which earns me some dap from Coach. In the game against Barringer, after I dish a sweet no-look to Larry streaking on the wing, Ray makes it a point to high-five me on the way back on defense. I stammer, trip as I turn to press the man bringing the ball up the court.

In the next timeout, Ray yells at the team to wake up and make some plays. Uses me as an example: JV actually looks up when he dribbles. Imagine that. Maybe other people could do the same.

And Coach agrees and weighs-in but his way of addressing the team is always a motivational speech that confuses us. Coach says things like: Broaden the ambit of your on-court persona. And: You are chimes, allow the wind to speak through you. Also: Let the emotion of the moment stir the sail of your soul. It's all stuff he's heard before, I'm sure. His mouth is a stream of words we'd have to look up but the horn goes off, the timeout is over, and his quotes are forgotten in our rush to get back on the court.

Some great evolution is taking place within me, in real time. I'm changing. Be a leader, I challenge myself. Be a leader, I repeat. I worry that the team needs more of me so I stress to myself the importance of making the right play. And at first I do. I make a timely assist; an extra pass that results in an easy bucket. I rotate on defense and surprise the ball handler; get a steal as a reward. But then, on offense, I jack up an ill-advised three and though Ray claps and tells me it's ok I know that it's not. Eager to cauterize my mistake, I try harder. I boss my bigs around, order them to post and pick, pick and post, flash, and Ray has the ball and he does what he does best. Net. Then he hits another. We close the gap. We're down by five.

The fourth quarter is easier, we're moving as a unit. Understanding not only our own roles but also those of our teammates. We understand where we are each going and where everyone else on the court is going. We play for where the ball is about to be. I'm feeling the rush. When I grip the ball we coalesce. A burst. I'm gone. My feet light as clouds, body weightless. Ray swings the ball to me and I drain a three to tie the game. Crowd goes off. We just need to hold them on the next possession. We know that and they know that. They halt the action at half-court to stress the importance of a good shot. They milk the clock. They try to look confident.

The ball comes into the paint but their big looks lost. We scramble, the ball comes back out to my man, I settle into my stance. He dribbles hard to the left and I'm expecting a pick to my right but the pick does not come. My man stops and pops. The ball is so clean it's pristine coming off his fingertips and we're down again, by two with eight seconds left.

We're out of timeouts. The ball inbounds to me and I race up the court and it feels like I'm in a different body because I'm leaving defenders in my wake like never before. A body count of a different sort. I think of Coach's words, though I don't know why they return to me now. I beat my man down the court. He's on my right hip, trailing, and I'm dribbling with my left hand. Full speed. A help defender shows. I come to a hard stop at the three-point line and absorb the contact from my defender, surprise him in doing so. I raise up and release, expecting a whistle to come. But the whistle doesn't come, and the ball follows its designated trajectory while the red seconds drain away like blood on the black scoreboard in the corner. I close my eyes. The horn sounds. We win by one.

Many things happen next but I see only a few.

1) Marcus comes up running from the bench with a towel draped over his shoulders and he isn't saying anything but his arms are fireworks spraying off in all directions.

2) Larry gives me a bear hug and lifts me up off the floor

as I pretend, with my demeanor, that I had no doubt about the shot.

Also:

3) Across the court, inexplicably open and with his arms still raised and his feet set, as if in some alternate universe another version of me might yet pass him the ball, Ray grimaces. But he's just the memory of a player who was open and I'm the momentary hero of the home crowd that has rushed the court.

For the next couple of days I reigned over that school, which is what happens when you hit a game-winning shot like I did. I capitalized on it, or tried to, because I knew the fame wouldn't last. High schools have the memory of goldfish, and sooner or later someone else, probably Ray, would come along and usurp the attention I now enjoyed. I talked to all the girls. All the girls. Even Sharon, who was in Ray's sights and should have been, according to the rules of etiquette that govern high school social life, off limits. I knew better, I really did. But Sharon had brown Colombian eyes that talked all the time so you couldn't be around her without a sense that some gravity was drawing you in. She looked at you and you felt emotionally undressed. She had eyes like that. That saw you. That talked. Whole paragraphs.

Ray saw us in the hallway, walking to class together, and Sharon was laughing at something stupid I'd said. Ray pulled up to us, on the other side of Sharon, and he wrapped his arm around her waist into a walking hug. He asked us what was so funny and Sharon started retelling my joke, which didn't sound as funny now that I heard it from her mouth, but I was happy that Sharon was laughing. Still, I was confused when she finished and Ray said he didn't get it. The joke wasn't that funny but it was at least mildly amusing. I tried to explain the joke, break it down: in my experience, a joke is always funnier when you explain it. But he still didn't get it and now we were single-file in the stairwell, headed down to lunch in the caf. I was in the front, with Sharon behind me and Ray behind her. I explained the joke in a different way but Ray still didn't find it funny.

We parked our trays at the usual table. Ray sat next to Sharon, across from me. Lunch was Salisbury Steak and, sensing an opening, I observed that Salisbury Steak is really just a long hamburger with different seasoning, but Ray didn't even budge. Not a smirk. Nothing.

In practice. Coach has us working on defensive footwork. It's a choreography of alphas with each player trying to win the possession for his side. The dance is subtle for the defender, a willing partner trying to wrest the lead away from the offensive player. The defender yearns to be first to a spot, to block the path, stop the progression of the offensive player. The music is all in the players' heads. In practice, we repeat the same steps until we all hear the same beat.

Ray is more engaged than I've ever seen him. He mops the court before practice and hustles on every play. He's early for shootaround and is the last to leave the locker room at the end of the day. I don't share this with anyone, but I'm convinced my game-winning shot has brought the best out of Ray. To see him like this, fueled by my success into a better version of himself, inspires me in turn, pushes me in similar fashion. I'm inspired by myself, in a sense. Strange. I think through the meaning of this and make yet another adjustment. Ray is now leading through his actions and less with the screaming and cajoling we've come to expect from him: a one-man version of a good-cop/bad-cop routine he inherited from the team captain before him. I think: I can fill this role. If Ray is the heart; I'll be the voice.

When Larry misses a rotation on defense I yell at him in my best Ray impersonation. It works. Larry nods and makes the adjustment. During a break in the action, Marcus asks me a question about feeding the ball into the post with the kind of spin that will bounce it in one direction but shoot it back up in another. I explain that it's all in the wrist, illustrate on the next possession. Coach shrugs, does not interject.

One of our bigs is slow to flash off a pick. I yell at him too. Announce that half-assing is beneath us. Ray is all work, happy to allow me the role of verbal enforcer. He moves with a blank stare that is like a sponge, accepting data but projecting nothing. I survey the court. We run the same play again. The dance resumes.

I go scoreless in the next game. Can't seem to get my legs under me. Still I fight. Get three steals. Five assists, four turnovers — not a good ratio. But we win. We're on the brink of making state. Next day, I'm early to practice but Ray is already there. Shooting jump shots by himself. I notice a slight modification in his form. At first, the change is hard to see but as I look more closely it's there and it's made his shot more closely resemble mine. I'm certain of this. It's in the angle of his elbow. I change quickly and make it on the court before anyone else arrives. I wonder if he'll say something. It's just us. I shoot at the opposite end. For the next twenty minutes, we're two strangers silently occupying the same court. When our teammates arrive, they cannot tell who has been there longer.

— // — // —

The next day I arrive early again and this time I actually

beat Ray to the gym. I change quickly, throwing my clothes in my bag instead of folding them like I usually do. Rushing out of the locker room I bump into Ray, who is just arriving for practice.

Huh, he says, moves quickly past me and around the corner behind the first row of lockers.

I grab a ball and start shooting. Each shot is contested, I imagine. Defenders and help defenders and rotating defenders. I see them all though they are not present. The ball rattles in each time and the basket looks as big as it's ever seemed to me. Ray comes on the court and starts shooting at my basket. It's only a matter of time until our individual drills sync and our shots arrive simultaneously. Both shots go in and we converge under the rim to retrieve our respective basketballs. I grab the one I think is mine.

This one's yours, he corrects.

We trade and I eye him with confusion. Then I catch myself and smile.

So you come down here early now?

I'm not sure what he means so I offer the only reply I can think of: Can never get in enough shots, you know?

Ray says nothing. He swallows. Dribbles away from me, looking down, which is a bad habit, but I don't correct him, just watch.

What do you think of the season? he asks. Then, when I hesitate: I mean, what do you think of how the team has been playing?

I rattle my brain for the answer but I pull up only echoes of phrases I've heard Coach say.

1) Defense has to get better.

2) Tighten up. Let's tighten this up right now.

3) Bad shots make bad teams.

I could say any of these but the context is wrong. I'm confused and my cheeks wash over in warmth I can't stop or control. I think some more.

4) Let's slow it down. Let's slow it down.

I say #2.

What? Ray asks.

I mean we're sloppy, I say. We're playing sloppy.

Maybe this is a good recovery. I don't know. I dribble at full speed in the opposite direction, careful to keep my head high as I make for the opposite end of the court. I can feel Ray's eyes following me, performing some kind of vigil I don't understand. I jack up a shot from thirty feet out but it's a brick and I chase the ball with shame while he follows me with a watchful gaze.

Before the next game, I decide that I'm going to look for Ray on every offensive possession. I tell no one about my plan. On our first possession, I bring the ball up the court and swing it to Ray. I go through the motion of cutting and shouting instructions and the ball comes back to me. I force a drive into the paint but practically really at Ray's defender, who falls for my ruse and collapses just enough to open the space I need. I pass the ball to Ray and he hits a jumper. It's a two because his foot was on the line and I'm disappointed that he's careless but it's not really that big a deal so I let it go.

On the next possession, I hand-off the ball to Ray as I set a pick on his man. He makes another shot and this time it is a three so I pump my fist and nod in his direction. He either doesn't see me or ignores me. He has no idea, clearly. Then Ray picks up two fouls, on consecutive possessions, no less, and he's on the bench. Silly fouls, too. I don't know what to do. The ball finds its way to me and I rack up a few buckets. The team goes on a run and when Ray returns to the court I return to my original strategy. I look for him every time up the court though Ray seems reluctant to shoot. I keep feeding him the ball, he keeps passing it to others. Always doing the right thing. He's exhausting.

Finally at half-time I ask him, point-blank in the locker room and before the entire team: Hey, Ray, are you going to shoot the fucking ball or what?

I don't realize it as I'm speaking but I'm actually shouting this question. Also, my tone is more aggressive than I intend it to be. Coach stares at me with a confused look and my teammates seem confused as well. Ray just stares at me. He's a carcass, not a real body.

In the third quarter, Ray picks up another foul and sits again. I grow frustrated and refuse to pass the ball. I take every shot. The ball doesn't leave my hands. Coach calls a timeout and I can sense I'm about to get my ass chewed out so I beat them all to the punch.

I declare: Man, take me out. I don't want to play with these fools no more.

$$- // - // -$$

After that, I think everyone on the team realized I was going through something. They didn't understand it, but they were aware. Before practice the next day, Ray was already shooting in the gym when Coach encouraged me to take the day off.

Go get some ice cream, he said. It was February.

Is this about yesterday? Because if so, I think I should really be back on the court to help us work through our issues. I was actually thinking about this last night and I have a solution. A very easy one, actually. We need more touches per possession. Swing the ball, move it around. Get everyone to buy in. Ray will agree.

Coach was distant. There was no kindle in his eyes when

he finally, plainly responded: Yes, this is about yesterday.

America is a free country, I said, like an alibi of sorts. Freedom of speech? Hello!?

Coach nodded as if I'd just confirmed something. He said: You were—he paused here, maybe for emphasis or maybe for clarity—impudent.

I shook my head and shrugged my shoulders with a cold chuckle. I didn't understand what he meant.

Go home, JV.

On my way out I didn't see Ray. The gym was empty.

$$— // — // —$$

I'm in first period English when Mrs. Ronson asks to see me in the hallway. She's my guidance counselor and so my English teacher obliges. Mrs. Ronson is tall with fingers like rulers that bend. Cherry-red lipstick. She's misleading in her politeness, a broad smile with an intimidating listen. She mines my words. Her eyebrows bob like the tracings on a polygraph.

I just want to make sure you're alright, she says. That there's nothing deeper going on between you and Ray. Because I've now heard multiple things from adults in the building, and I just spoke to Ray and he doesn't understand what's going on. So are we good? Are you guys good? Or is something going on? What's the beef, JV?

I don't know which question to answer. I focus, explain to her how the season is very stressful on players, and how Ray is managing the additional stress of preparing for college. I say to her: Maybe me and Ray just need a good heart-to-heart. Man to man.

I hate myself for offering this, for how I sound, but I say it before I fully consider the implications. I'm relieved when she dismisses the suggestion.

She says: I think that for the time being it's probably best that you keep your distance from Ray. Can I trust you to do that?

During practice that day I say nothing. Larry makes a mistake: I don't correct him. Marcus shows up late: not my problem. The rage in my belly is a fire no more, is the sun at dusk and I am happy to observe in silence. On a few occasions Coach tries to coax me into volunteering an opinion. What do you think? he asks at one point. I don't know, I say. And I don't know. The team is watching me and I don't see Ray. The walls look too far from where I'm standing, as if the court has expanded while I wasn't paying attention. Coach tries again: Are you sure? Nope, I confirm.

Probably best not to stretch beyond my current enclosures, I reason to myself, once Coach restarts the action. I feel inspired by the unexpected peace I find in surrendering my responsibilities. My entire being is lighter. Once practice ends Ray and the others go in the locker room but I leave without changing back into my street clothes.

From then on I proceed as if I'm in the witness protection program. I'm careful, reserved. I'm a wallflower. A tacit tactician. My life becomes a muted movie and I perfect, with an ease greater than I could have expected, the ability to tune out the world. More than once over the next few days I glance up at someone who is standing beside me, speaking to me, frustrated at my distraction.

I'm sorry, I say, simply and devoid of emotion. I didn't hear you just now.

— // — // —

But my approach is soon tested: in History class, I get paired with Sharon for a team project. I have kept my distance from the world but now I'm required to engage. Sharon suggests we meet on Saturday. I'm reawakened. Her voice is an elixir and her laugh reverbs inside my head at night. She knows me, I think. Like she really sees me, understands everything.

She's already sitting at a small table for two when I arrive at the coffee shop across from the high school on New York Ave. She looks softer up close. Her eyes are dimmer but no less potent, a vestige of doubt I can't explain. While she speaks I study the make-up she has brushed horizontally across her cheek. I study those cheekbones, wider than her jaw. The analysis dilutes some of the magic about her but I find myself more drawn to her now than I was before. More amazement than interest. She's more real, too real, and I feel more at ease than I have in weeks. It's as if all the words I've been saving up during that time are suddenly at my full disposal.

She smiles, asks: What?

Caught, I shrug and say: I was thinking about this project. And then I redirect the conversation.

The hours pass and I can smell the caffeine on her breath, reaching across the short distance between us to draw out my secrets.

How's the season going? she asks.

It's good. If we win the next game we'll be in good shape.

I can't believe how you hit that game-winner against Barringer. The guy was draped over your back.

You were at that game?

Of course.

I don't remember seeing her, but that entire game is a blur.

Talking to her is so easy, like she already knows what I'm going to say.

She probes: You were double-teamed. Why didn't you pass the ball?

I think of Ray, open across the court while I forced up a shot. I swallow hard.

I say: I really don't know. Sometimes when I play, I'm not really thinking. I'll make a move or run a play out of instinct. I don't know the play is going to happen until after it's happened. I've done it so many times that my body reacts faster than my mind can process. It's muscle memory.

So is that what you guys practice? Is that why you spend hours and hours and days and months locked in a musty gym?

She's teasing. I smile politely.

I mean, yes, but it's not just practice. Every game, pick-up or official, is a chance to repeat my habits. The good ones *and* the bad ones. It's all so I get to a point where I make the right play, every time.

I see.

And there's more. Practice teaches how to read opposing players and make judgments based on what I'm seeing. A great shooter might be struggling that day, and I adjust because doing so grants me an advantage over my opponent. Basketball is a game of duels. And I learn to do that, to read those subtleties, through practice.

Sounds like you're training your body *and* your mind.

That's it. If I eliminate the extraneous, movements not needed, then it's like unlocking a shortcut. I'll be the first to a spot. The first to react, the fastest on the court. That's the goal.

To be the best.

Of course. Part of it is convincing yourself.

That you're the best.

I nod, declaim: Buy into the conceit that you are a superior player, or crumble into your own relevance.

She laughs, tilts her head with mild uncertainty in her eyes.

That's something Coach says. I can't claim credit for it.

Good, I was starting to worry.

Don't worry.

So it's not all pick-up games, huh?

I assure her: Oh, there are plenty of pick-up games.

Where?

Somewhere.

Ah, so it's one court. A special court.

Each player has a special court.

She smiles: *Your* special court.

Any player worth his salt has a special court. Like a secret.

Ah, a lair.

Of sorts.

There are no secrets in this city, JV, just confusion about what others actually know.

So I'm learning.

So? Where is your lair?

And then I'm telling her, without really knowing why I'm doing it: St Charles Street. Behind the ice-skating rink. The rims are tight but not too much. A few cracks on the asphalt but they're thin. And the surface is even. That's very important. Very important. It's where I play. The court always attracts the same faces. There are the weekday evening faces, and the weekend faces.

Like a schedule.

Sort of. You start to follow the same schedule as the crew you play with. You learn their games, they learn yours. You learn the rules: first to seven wins, winner stays for two games max. You run games up and down the court and the hours fall away. Whole years pass like skins you've shed.

But you've only been here a few months.

In some ways, different city same court. Before this one it was another one.

I see. But now it's this one.

I've moved a lot. First thing I do at a new place is find a new court. Once I find that, place feels more mine than before.

She's listening with her entire being. Her eyes are full blast. I read in them curiosity, maybe something more I don't recognize, so I continue.

One time, I was playing in one of the summer tournament games with the AAU team. Their point guard was like 6'5 and our coach thought I should just take him 'cause I'm the point guard, so this 6'5 point guard is thinking he's just going to score in the paint. First play, he posts me up and when the ball comes he dribbles twice to back me up and gets a layup. Nothing I could do, right? Next possession, he doesn't even give up the ball. He just turns and backs me down, another lay-up. The coach is looking at me like I'm supposed to do something about this but I can't stop the guy.

What?

Yeah. The coach says it's my problem. Next possession is more of the same but now I've got to try something different. So I put all of my weight up against this guy, I mean I really go at him, and I surprise him at first. He hesitates, then smirks, takes one hard dribble and bumps me off the spot. I lean my weight up against him once more and he starts to dribble again. But just as he moves back with the ball I slide out of the way.

She laughs.

I pulled the chair out from under him and he came tumbling down. He was expecting me there, to fight. But the absence of contact threw him off balance and he fell so hard on his ass. Everyone laughed. He complained his lower back hurt and he threw a fit asking for a foul but there was no foul. He went to the bench and didn't come back in the game. Trainers put ice on his back but the bruise was elsewhere.

Sharon's eyes are still smiling but there's confusion in them, too.

His pride, I explain. It was his pride that was hurt, not his back.

She nods. After she taps briefly on her phone we leave together. We don't get two blocks before we run into Ray.

He's wearing black track pants and a hoodie, hands in his pockets, and he says: Hey, Sharon.

That might have been the strangest walk of my life. Ray was a sentinel, saying nothing as we walked. I remember his posture and how I wanted to be restrained, thinking about Mrs. Ronson and her warning, and of Coach forcing me to take a day off. I must have seemed so odd. Sharon tried to regenerate our conversation by talking about our history project. I started to answer but then even that felt dangerous, like I was volunteering information that could later be used against me. I stopped.

I was convinced Ray had come to confront me about my behavior. Coach and Ronson, they were just the first volleys, I figured. I started to think of comebacks, things I could say if Ray said something to me. I tried to catch him out of the corner of my eye but he was only a silhouette of an intruder, a surly enforcer reluctant to take up his task. He didn't return my look. I don't remember him looking in my direction even once. I was grateful.

We kept walking and soon we arrived at the corner of Lafayette where I knew Sharon would turn left to go home.

Alright, guys, I said, turning right. I'll see you later.

Sharon chuckled. Her eyes emitted a signal in a language I did not understand. She looked like she wanted me to say something else.

I have to stop at ShopMart, I lied, but it was a lie woven out of desperation. Forgivable, I imagined.

Ray stared off to our left, down the block in the direction where he would now walk Sharon home. I waved again. Sharon stared at me a second longer, then waved back.

Thanks, JV, she said, deflated, turning to join Ray.

After they had crossed the street, I cupped my hands and shouted: Don't worry guys. Everything is going to be just fine.

I deliver a phenomenal presentation in History. Mr. Freese commends me and Sharon looks thrilled, if distant. She's standing directly next to me but she's miles away, too, and I'm focused. Ray sits in the back of the class, watching me. He is not clapping; all the other students are clapping. Inspiration strikes. In an instant, I have my next move plotted out so clearly I can't wait to get started.

The plan: instead of going to last period, I will wait in the gym. I could probably just race down there when the bell rings but I don't want to chance it. Ray will be there promptly to start his shootaround and though recently I've beaten him to the gym on more than a few occasions, today I want to watch him as he starts his routine. I have questions I need answered.

1) What does Ray do when no one is watching?

2) Is Ray's routine any different when no one is watching?

3) What secrets is Ray keeping from me, from the rest of the team?

Ray strikes me as someone who keeps secrets.

4) Who, really, is Raymond Frye?

I'm turning a corner on the third floor when I spot Mrs. Ronson at the far end of the hallway, talking to a teacher. She turns quickly when she hears my footsteps. She announces a generic, Get to class, which lets me know she didn't see me. I back-tracked in time. Still, that was too close. I can't afford to be caught.

I sneak around, back up to the fourth floor and then take the back stairwell all the way down to the first level. Snaking up the stairs to the veranda outside the coaches' offices I see some students coming late to gym class; I pass unnoticed. The offices are closed during the school day. With no one around, this is the perfect place to wait out the period. I prepare my notebook, find a fresh page and write the title across the top: Observation Log, 2 March. I doodle along the left margin waiting for the time to pass, then, once I've exhausted that space, I write Ray's name on the first line. At the end of the period, the bell rings and I sense the flicker in my stomach. The time is now.

Within two minutes, Ray enters the gym and he's only in the locker room for about a minute or so. Then he's outside in his warm-ups and I hear him dribbling a ball. He jogs to the other end of the court and then there's silence. I gamble a peek. He's stretching, holding the ball with both hands and bending at the waist. Then he's stretching his calves and warming up his knees.

Ray takes jumpers from the foul line, then moves to the elbows. At first he's shooting in place but within a few minutes he's dribbling into his shots. Unprovoked, he picks up the intensity. He's clasping his rebounds with grunts and taking them right back up. He's running around the court and jacking up shots. On a long rebound he chases the ball to half-court and proceeds in that trajectory at full speed before throwing down a dunk with both hands. He hangs on the rim for a moment, then grabs the ball and dunks it again. He's really loud now. Eventually he grabs the ball and kneels. He's very still for a while, his slumped shoulders up and down like a tide coming in. Then I hear sobs. He's wiping at his face and I realize it's not sweat he's wiping. I don't know why I do it, I don't know that I'm going to do it, — surprise, maybe?— but I laugh. I laugh loud. Ray hears me. Hides his face even as he shouts, Who's there?

I race out of there as fast as I can. I have with me the Observation Log but I don't know what I've done with my pen. Doesn't matter. A non-descript Bic, blue ink. Ray won't make me from that.

I give it a while before I go back. I walk around the block to the Portuguese bakery. Grab a Gatorade and a butter roll. A celebratory meal. When I walk into the gym, practice is already under way. Coach follows me into the locker room. I'm putting on my sneakers when I see him standing there. He looks embittered, pondering a conversation I don't yet know we're about to have.

Can I talk to you for a second?

Sure, Coach.

Look, I'll just cut to the chase — were you spying on Ray's shootaround today?

What?

Were you outside my office today, on the veranda, watching Ray shoot around?

I can't imagine how Coach knows. Did Ray make me from my laugh? Did he see me? I steel myself for what I'm about to say: Coach, you know. Ray was crying. I don't think he is well. He needs help.

Coach closes his eyes, takes a deep breath: JV, why were you spying on Ray?

He's been acting very strangely, we all know that. And he's been following me.

He's following *you*?

Well, one time he followed me, on a Saturday, but I can't be sure. He might have been there for Sharon.

Sharon Martinez?

Yes.

You're not making any sense. Why is she involved?

We delivered a phenomenal presentation in History, you can ask Mr. Freese, and all the students in the class clapped for us except Ray. He just sat in the back and did not clap. Like a psychopath. It was very disconcerting and, you know, he needs help

JV, this doesn't make any sense.

I know, Coach. I don't understand this any more than you do. It's very strange.

JV, I think you're obsessed with Ray.

Obsessed? He's the one who's obsessed with me. Clearly. I just explained this to you. Are you listening to me? He shows up unexpectedly. He doesn't talk to me.

Coach shakes his head.

He didn't clap for us, Coach.

Mrs. Ronson said it would come to this and, honestly, I've been hoping she'd be wrong..

I know, Ray's not well, Coach. It's very sad and we have to support him. All of us. The team.

Coach touches his right temple: I think it's best if you leave the team.

What? Are you listening to anything I'm saying?

You need some time, and we're going to get Mrs. Ronson involved so you can get what you need, but you're done here.

Coach.

I'm sorry, JV. I really am.

But Coach, I'm a victim here. Ray is the aggressor.

Coach remains, still as a wreck, but I'm the one who's sinking. All around me the lockers are rising and the floor is coming up on me like liquid abandonment. How will I explain this to Marie at home? She's been so good to me and I've been good in return. Honest. But getting kicked off the team is too far. Maybe she'll send me back.

I stay in place for what seems like a long time. I wait for Coach to leave but he's waiting for me to leave and I can't move. The floor is still rising, at my waist now and my peripherals are hazy. A light flickers in the corner but I can't afford to look away from Coach right now.

Marcus enters the locker room. He looks in our direction but doesn't break stride on his way to the urinal. I take a final breath, then I'm under but there are no bubbles, just a rubbery heaviness that swallows me from the inside.

$$-\,//-//-$$

When my doorbell rang that evening I was in my room. I didn't think much of it until Mrs. Ronson walked in as I sat on the bed, Marie diagonally to her left in the doorway. Ronson didn't stay long but she talked and I nodded. At everything.

Marie watched, silently, doubt flickering at first but fading away eventually. It was just me on the bed and they were speaking at me from a great distance. I wasn't distressed, just tired.

Ronson spoke very slowly that evening: So you can keep going to school, but you have to meet with me and Mr. Spencer.

Who's Mr. Spencer?

A specialist.

Ok.

And you're off the team. For good. You are not to attend practice or any of the games.

I nodded. I think I kept nodding even after she left. The

world was demanding something of me and I just had to agree. Survival I knew well.

— // — // —

In addition to practice and games, I'm also not to address Ray in any way. I'm moved to a different lunch and History class. My new History teacher is Ms. Quach, who my classmates had in freshman year but she's gotten worse, they say. She talks to the chalk when we refuse to answer her discussion questions. She calls the chalk Mr. White.

Mr. White, what do you think? she asks it.

There's only the gentle murmur of other classes coming from the hallway but she listens intently to a reply no one else hears. It's hard to watch.

I open my notebook and I'm staring at the Observation Log from 2 March. I marvel at my detailed notes because I don't remember making them. How did I manage to simultaneously watch Ray and write so neatly? And why is the blue ink in the notes different from the blue ink in the title and on the doodles in the margin? I remember Ray's sobbing that day. Why would he have been sobbing? And then I'm sad, for the first time, because Ray is probably someone who is in deep pain and no one knows. Ray isn't getting the help he needs even though everyone thinks he has the city in the palm of his hand: a four-year scholarship to a D1 program, the fame that comes with being a star athlete, the adoration — Ray has all that people pray for when they pray for their wishes to come true.

Though I am a spectacle in the building, I feel for Ray. He is a tragic figure, undoubtedly aware of his illegitimate reign at the helm of the team. Terrified of it, I am sure. It is so obvious. Ray has nowhere to hide now. Very soon, he will be revealed as a fraud. Immediately I wonder what I can do to help him.

The convalescence begins. In my first session with Mrs. Ronson, Mr. Spencer mainly watches. I hear his voice only as a hello and then as a goodbye. A human boomerang in a sports coat. They're here, trying to fix me, and Ray is out there alone, feeling the crushing weight of the crowd's expectations during the final of the County Tournament. And I'm not there to help him.

Spencer and Ronson get from me the answers I know they want and I can sense in them the inference that maybe I won't prove as difficult a case as they'd presumed. Survival I know well.

That night, I write one letter to Coach and one letter to Mrs. Ronson. Marie asks me to leave them on the kitchen table, says she'll read them after she finishes the dishes. Before bed, I grab some water out of the fridge and see the letters still folded on the kitchen table. She's watching her shows so I don't want to disturb her. The next morning I ask Marie what she thinks of them and she says, They're fine.

I drop the letters off in the main office, in the respective cubbies on the wall with the staff mailboxes. I know what I need to do. I recommit myself to my ultimate goal, the principles that matter and I make a decision not to tolerate distractions. I'll ghost. Work on my own. Perfect my game. Excellence will be my vocation, in time my legacy. Then they won't deny me.

I say to myself: imagine the harvest that is yours and sow your way to it.

— // — // —

I have the St Charles court to myself. My basketball is my shield though I wield it like a weapon. Each dribble is a singular struggle for position; each shot is a stroke that lands.

My form is flawless. I remember Ray's modified jumpshot. Ray shooting in the gym, at that very moment, a playoff game underway. Outdoor shooting is unique. The ball behaves differently. I focus on my feet, my balance, feet under me and determined when I step or jump or slide. I am a trained soldier. I defend when the time comes. On offense, I am methodical. A machine programmed to get buckets. Get buckets.

I make a list of my strengths as a player. Passing is first, of course. Ray is a lesser passer. He doesn't see the game the same way I do. He hasn't trained his eyes like I have trained my eyes so that even as I'm making a move into the paint, I am aware. I am conscious of my teammates' positions. I know where they are. I know where they are going. I am one with the court.

I grab a rebound. The air is vast beneath my feet though I feel the height mainly in my knees. I'm at the edge of a cliff and I'm past the edge but I haven't jumped. I linger at the apex of my jump before descending. I turn and race up the court on an imagined fast break. I picture Marcus to my right and Larry on my left, filling the lanes. My other teammates are there, too, even Coach on the sideline. I see them though they are not present. All of them. Even Ray, who is on defense, I imagine. Ray is on the other team. Ray is the only defender back and we're barreling toward him at the height of our speed. Ray is on his heels. Ray is looking around for help. We're in the paint and I go right into his chest, to the lip of the rim. I score.

Another fast break. This time going the other way and Ray is livid because he's the only one back again. I'm breathing heavily but I see the frustration on his face and it drives me forth. Ray tries to draw a charge but I smell it coming and release the ball to Marcus, slide just past Ray's clenched form, and Marcus throws down a dunk.

Now it's not a fast break. One on one. Provoked, Ray

wants retribution. A duel. I dribble. He wants to prove he can stop me and he's playing me at an angle to try to force me left. But Ray should know better. Ray should know that going left is my strength. I briefly consider putting a crossover through his legs; with a stance that wide it's what he deserves. But I rise up and drain a three in his grill. Water.

I say: Go rinse that out, Ray.

At the top of the key, I hit him with one hard dribble to the right then a pull-up at the elbow. True. A dirge for who he once was. I don't understand why I am treating him this way, though I am very aware of how good it feels.

I say: You're not the star, Ray.

If I make another shot, I think, I'll tell him all the things I've been meaning to say. A green pick-up trundles down the street and I take my first dribble. I'm going right at Ray. Our movement is a poem, an enjambment of limbs — where one ends being not where the other begins. I put the ball through my legs, hesitate, bring the ball back with another crossover backward through the legs. I tell Ray: Focus, the real move is coming now. I pause at the top, align my hips, then I'm past him but he grabs my shorts so I swing my elbow behind me. The layup goes in and I'm in his face.

1) You were never shit, Ray.

2) You never gave me a shot, Ray.

3) You're going to fall apart without me, Ray, because you know you need me.

I'm spitting my words, the saliva sticks to my chin.

4) I fucking hate you, Ray.

Then I'm grabbing the ball and starting another fast break because I'm the fastest player on the team and no one is going to beat me down the court.

But I dribble only once before I stop. Someone not imagined is watching by the gate. He is real. I don't know how long he's been there or what he's heard me say, but I recognize him in those black track pants and a hoodie, hands in his pockets. I wonder why he has come to see me when he has a game to play. I wonder what excuse he has used to escape the expectations. And I wonder what versions of a tomorrow are unraveling for him now that he has traveled so far to find me on this court, of all places.

ROBIN MOVED IN

Robin moved in with her clothes and her toiletries and her mother's silver necklace that she never wore for fear of ruining or breaking or losing it. And the cat, too.

The few job interviews I had weren't calling back and I was nervous without letting her know. It was her name on the checks to the rent and the cable and the gas. I paid the electric, mostly.

We had been in the kitchen that first night when I said to her soft almond eyes, "I'll do the dishes." She answered, "OK," in a half-whisper and that was when I first knew we'd be ok, somehow, in the small apartment that was suddenly ours. And the cat's.

Now she's bedridden and doesn't know her own name, and I drag my stubborn feet when I walk, but we had a good life in between then and now.

STILL LIFE

She opens her eyes and checks the time. Deliberate, how the hands move to mark the passing of the firsts. A ritual, their suicide. If change has meaning time must be its marker. But now, ok. This clock knows only the oldest of phrases. Not even the shield of Achilles can match its truths.

The morning, though, is a separate beast. Her bones, contradicted, complain of the chaos. They don't want to step one two. They crave authority. Autonomy? A monotonous monogamy of peace. Still the darkness recedes. Something must rise to fill its void. She moves with cautious purpose. A majority of one.

In the mirror, swollen memories: ornaments not disturbed. They wash away in water once distant and remote. Polite house guest. Arriving then leaving. The drain does its part.

Her mouth bleeds again. She spits. Time for a new brush. Time for a new brush. Water.

Time for a new brush. In the hall her feet fall firm like practiced, one two ok now three four and there's the kitchen. Blooming to welcome her arrival. It's just another morning but ask the dead about the sun-up. Expired in the rising. Still, has she not died in manners smaller if not less frequent? She knows not to expect, that satisfaction is a bruise to carry no different than grief. It, too, a memory. Would there was a drain for that, too.

She glances through the window. Bright world bright. The season is new but the foliage is old. There's no reverence for its brittle colors. Already forgotten: the discrete cover of its shade. She remembers summers at the city pool — first her own then as a parent. Those years long submerged. She preserves the act of remembering. Prolonging only the smallest of its magic seems hardly adequate. She furnishes first the sounds but then, with the images, the doors to the changing rooms become the doors to the high school gymnasium.

Could objects have second lives? She bargains with herself but the response is more silence. Those boys had names. Hers? Outside her body the world renews as outside the window: an early orgasm of light. Who wouldn't court desire if inclination was outcome?

She averts her eyes.

In the cupboard, there are mugs in a mug there is coffee now. She brings closer her nose for inspection. What, should she suspect the smell radiating like a sound? She shushes the thought. Shh. In the living room, she speculates on the age of a pot. Shhhhh. The thin plant is idle and so many conceive of life strictly as motion. Foreign; an alternate understanding. Many would agree with many, not with her. But there is motion that escapes the eye. Too. She knows, and if there is motion maybe she too is moving now. Motion: of ideas, for one; of emotions, two. And we've covered already the memories — the motion of memories that go. And return, maybe. Trailing contradictions, they are. The coffee is strong. But shhh.

She is a woman of many lives. She knows. Many live the same life, not her. She never found her wharf. Every turn a new dock. She, who never learned how to tread, only swim, what does that symbolize? A symbol is a meaningful way to represent. From the minor inferred the major; all is told from the small. The couch is stifling. She sits. Wrestles for a space, settles. Doing so is a translation familiar. Was there a warning she missed? If the first time she had come to this couch there had been another to warn her perhaps life might not have progressed this way.

There was happiness, she knows.

Happiness she knows. Days made up of entire years and how she treasured those. How faintly they escaped. What Christmas cookies were those she recalls now? She moved into the apartment in 1983. The neighborhood quite different then. Did she take the cookies to which neighbors? Moats separate those realities. All existed and that much is clear. The order is the problem. Confusion. That other language.

Life is what happened while she was doing things numerous. Her husband dead ten years and still she feels his orbit. The distance between them greater but the pull is the same. It knows her ways. First she grieved him because she missed him, later she feared him because she forgot his departure. Or was it return? And what would she do with him now? Time does that, too. We rely on words but the body has a language its own. She would pick up all the words, across languages vast and distinct, but she bit her right index nail too far. Restraint is a virtue she remembers only after the fact and now the cold is in the coffee. The thermostat!

She presses twice on the plus and the numbers they change. She makes the bed after the kitchen and the dishes washed away. She is too small for this mass. Still: stretch the sheets. Love is dedication, simply put. Does she love these sheets? What else could she call her life? She does not cry when the scent finds her senses. Lavender. A quiet consolation. She is reconciled. His affair was a diversion, after all. The real issues were what wasn't and she came to see that once it was there again. Later. How avidly he admired her bone structure beautiful long after the gloaming of conceiving of herself as such. Good. The power she recovered. That there was kindness with those burdens. A paradox. A dictionary for existence. Abridged, though enough. She had received him and then the boys. Lives since diverted, hers included. And now memory is just her reminder of what's gone. Or is it an exercise in the alternate?

At lunch she almost eats a fresh tomato. She tramples her way through the meal. Moves all the pieces but consumes less. Contact is a reward and she enjoys the pageantry of colors. Click clack the reds and greens around the white moon. An effigy of the natural order. Oh yes to the small pleasures she learned once. And the school bus loudly in the street. Is it already the hour? Miniature people who mistake existence for what they've seen. She witnesses through sheer curtains. Perspective chiseled away at her over the seasons and the ceiling of her understanding vaulted vaulted vaulted. Vaulted. In some cases experience was supplanted once acquired. She smiles different. But those eager feet slapping the pavement just outside her front door are an applause of sorts. She did the same. The recollection of the feeling is hers too.

The stifle from the walls is a repetition. She considered escape, briefly, then repeatedly. Her mettle was never to start again. So she continued as now she observes the cars where they go. Far as she can see them exit. They don't stop there and isn't that just the way of the universe? The lightening and darkening of the corners despite us. She plays a hymn. Just a few buttons pressed and her walls are breached. Autumn Leaves. She smiles? No. She touches her cheek where another once grazed it. A token of a moment still happening somewhere. There is a family of syllables to explain those things that exist but can't be held. And there is a weight to them, she nods, though she has not a scale to fit the task.

Here comes what she has been expecting. At last. A painting. Brush strokes: violent. Tones: broken Earth. Earthy. But broken. Like light. Like life. She's really going now, getting there. So close that the painting is her, for her, about her. But the apartment remains like parentheses. And she's multiple but singular. Her migration is not physical. She is an accomplice to herself and someone has turned on the light. A flick of the switch. That's not magic, that's science, but once it was magic. Magical. Still? She doesn't wish to consider that. There is the painting, yes, still the painting. Her feet tread one of the strokes first then another second. She is small though the order continues. She progresses and the rest desists. She would have this as a vocation. As hers. Possession.

Eyes closed and the tune repeats. Arrivals supplement do not supplant. The echoes of herself reverb here — safe and rustic. A perimeter emerges and she sees the containers of existence. Some. There are clothes to fold. Their cleanliness is inspiration. Lavender: where has she smelled that before? She pulls a book from the shelves, later. Red spine. How does this one middle? She can't remember the build-up. And she despises spectacles. Much better to surprise. As in experience. Within, like parentheses. Pages and pages. Why try to explain? Who will come seeking understanding? When?

Again she mingles. With the furniture. Flanking first then another. The redesign of the same pieces to illusion change. Transformation is too much. Much, too. Before bed, per ritual, she finds the picture of the four. She is one. The others already told. Considered. Absent now. Maybe for good. Peace is an absence, too. She breathes. Not for the first time but for the first conscious instance in many breaths. All the things we do without deliberation. Conviction warrants consideration. This is different. Much easier to draw back the blankets, fix the pillows. Before sleep one last memory: of praying for safe-keeping. A nameless angel to watch over a girl. So she was raised.

Finally she is ready. A closing of sorts. And yet so much that is and isn't, moves and doesn't, exists despite. Overwhelming for some. She manages. A corner all her own, that's the way. Distant from the tumult there is a silence that finds her. She has to listen for it. Intent on stillness, is this the her she should be? Eyes closing now. Shh shhhh shh, she goes shhhhhhhh. Shh! But she doesn't. She isn't moving in her bed. In the cave of her sheets not very much at all. Life. A life. Is. Is still.

THE DAY MY FATHER DECIDED TO DIE

First thing that morning, shirtless and in a cotton shower skirt, he downed a shot of port wine and smoked a cigarette. On the TV, an anchorwoman mouthed important updates he would not need to know.

The first time he breakfasted this way, as a boy of fifteen, there was such freedom in his choice. There was, too, a wisp of manhood that he relished.

I imagine he saw this routine as a bad habit he could finally be rid of. An unfit punishment for living — the same breakfast, day after day, for thirty five years.

That last morning, did he think of the origin? Did he rue the sweetness of that first morning's taste? Did he finally realize that he had been trying to kill himself even back then, even before he finally up and did it?

OUTSIDE IN

The buzzer opening the gate is an alarm clock releasing him from a hazy dream where he's stumbled from meal to meal and check to check. Just after eleven in the morning and the sky above him is real not like the sky above the yard but a real sky he can almost touch. He can smell it, too, the sky, and he remembers the city he hasn't seen in so long.

He steps forward. The pavement is a stretch of blacktop poured over a packed dirt and pebble path, barely onced over with a paver. To his right and left the way stretches toward nowhere. This is the forgotten edge of town. Though there are no buildings or people, just cars scattered across a too big parking lot, this is the world. Again. At last. Wallless and infinite.

Across the way a man in dark denim jacket and pants nods in his direction then waves past him to a guard watching from the other side of the 15 foot fence. He looks back at the guard, then both ways before walking over to the man in denim, who asks him, They tell you 'bout me?

He goes, Yeah, they told me.

So you ready? You good with the rules?

Yeah, I'm good.

Aight. Just needed to hear you say it.

They drive toward the city dodging pot holes. Discarded trash decomposes on the side of the road. The drive is warehouses and abandoned factories, at first, then truck repair shops and depots, and then surely enough come some homes and streetlights, then more of both, and eventually the city as a different version of a place he remembers. He stares blankly at his off-center reflection in the sideview mirror. His eyes are empty obsidian, a bleary white spot at the edge of the pupil to impersonate a life. This is freedom, he thinks.

He begins to recognize some of the buildings as they approach downtown, though the streets around them have been reconfigured. He turns back over his shoulder to look at the unemployment office building on Broad. It has a line that snaketails out of the door and around the front and side of the building.

Yeah, says the man in denim, lots of unemployed.

He offers no response so the man in denim goes on. Yeah, they talk 'bout all the business that's coming back to the city. Like it's a sign that things is better. They call it investin in urban areas, but it's all big companies comin here for cheap labor. They set up shop. Low prices. And they pay minimum wage and drive out the few small businesses that's still left. Only a few of 'em these days.

The man in denim pauses to see whether he's going to speak but he just stares ahead.

They drainin the rest of the blood, the man in denim adds. Soon there won't be none left. Which is why people need religion more than ever.

The side streets are quiet. The Caprice hums peacefully at a red light. Then red turns green, grants them passage, and they drive again.

How long you was in for? the man in denim asks. As a rule, the man in denim pulls hard on the steering wheel but the big body Caprice seems used to the treatment. It hugs the curves with only a slight sway.

Seven years.

For what?

Crime.

The man in denim stares him down, the car maintains its speed. What kind of crime?

The illegal kind.

You wanna fuck around we can go back.

A pause, then a submission: I don't wanna talk about what I did before I went in. Don't matter.

It matter to me, the man in denim persists.

He offers no reply. The man in denim pulls fast on the

124

wheel and kicks the brake to pull over the Caprice.

He turns his head toward the man in denim. He does at least that.

Yo, the man in denim goes on, this ain't how it gonna work, my dude. The man in denim lets the pause hang in the air for a second, like a threat. You wanna go back in I take you back and they just send me somebody else. Same difference to me. Now, you either gonna answer when I talk to you or this shit ends right here.

He thinks of the food inside and the cramped space and the same faces day after day and about how tired he is of it all. He remembers how this was described to him, A new beginning.

I caught a body, he offers.

The man in denim nods. I knew you was a hard one, the man in denim says, pulling the car out of its spot without sympathy. But even hard ones gotta obey.

They drive across the city some more. Streets pass like memories.

You hungry?

I could eat, he says.

They pull up to Jimmy Buff's on 14th and 9th, or the place that used to be Jimmy Buff's when he was last here. He is glad that the man in denim orders for the both of them, Italian dog with the works, because even the ten item menu displayed on a large blackboard above the counter is a demanding thing with its options and descriptions requiring a choice. He finds himself looking around with the same intensity of eating inside where he kept his head on a swivel, always on a swivel, but they are the only two customers in the place and the eat-in tables feel small as he struggles to find comfort in the cramped silence of the place. He takes the seat facing the door. Sizzling behind the counter and smoke rising above and around the glass enclosing the grill. He thinks of how inside he saved packets of peanut butter and jelly to use with other meals later on — in the real world, he remembers with stoic amazement, he can just ask for more ketchup if he wants it, or extra salt. But how would he ask? Would he have to walk up to the counter? Ask for it as he grabbed his food? Whatever, he can cross that bridge later. It's the little freedoms that give you back your humanity, he thinks, but maybe it's too early to tell.

He eats way too fast and looks up to find the man in denim watching him. He notices that one of the man in denim's ears is lower than the other. The lack of symmetry strikes him as a strange thing and he stares an instant too long. He wipes his mouth on the back of his hand.

Aight. The man in denim takes a bite of his Italian dog with the works. Nods while chewing, gives a look like an idea has just come but this isn't a man to be ambushed by an idea.

Behind the counter one of the workers scrapes the grill.

So I know they told you 'bout me, but how much they told you 'bout how this works?

He focuses on the man in denim. It's best you just tell me everything now so I'm clear.

Fair enough. The man in denim pauses. Then: This a re-entry program. We understand you been inside for... how long, again?

Seven years.

Right. Well, the world change in that time. I make sure your re-entry goes smooth. You know, they done studies that show that even using money and rememberin to eat is difficult for former convicts. You gettin a second chance now, so we wanna make sure this works for you. That you adjust to life outside, so to speak.

Yeah, I get that's the story. But what's we really doin me and you?

The man in denim raises his brows. Fair enough. I like that. Directness. I like that. The man in denim goes to speak but then clouds gather over what was about to be said and the man in denim does not speak. The man in denim is sizing him up, again, with eyes that squint to zoom, see deeper. The man in denim sees a man just now freed on parole after seven years inside and then goes to speak again but says only, That's a great question. The man in denim takes another bite to build suspense or whatever the fuck is about to happen, watches him from across the table with the food being chewed and considered. Then the man in denim wipes away some extra ketchup with a paper napkin and focuses on him one more time. He feels the weight of the look he's getting from the man in denim. I like that, the man in denim repeats before taking another bite.

He knows better than to look away or show a reaction. Even his blinking is measured. For all he knows the man in denim is a cop, or a former cop. This man in denim running this experimental parole program. This man in denim making him wait for an answer to a simple question. But the waiting is a test, too, in a way, and he knows that. That's alright, he can wait. He waits. He can wait. For years he's done nothing but wait. If not for this, he'd still be waiting.

We gonna try it today, the man finally says. You gonna see for yourself. We gonna... help you adjust.

Adjust?

Yeah, you know. Put your skills to some purposeful use.

He knows what this means, what he already knew it meant. He's playing a game, now, with this man in denim, but it's a game whose rules are not known to him and still he has no choice but to play. To refuse is to go back in and he doesn't want that. Not at all. During his time he's seen too many be released only to come back a few months, or even weeks, later. Men who no longer understand freedom, don't know who else to be. He's promised himself that he won't go down the same road as those men. So he says nothing. He is an empty wall and the man in denim's words advance in his direction.

We gonna try it today and if you can make this work we gonna keep going. For one week, the man in denim holds up his right index finger, Or until you can't make it work no more.

And if I make it work?

Then, the man in denim emphasizes, you get your release. And once that happen I'ma check in with you every week or so, make sure you still makin it work, and if you can keep makin it work we won't have no problems.

OK, he says. He knows there's more here than he's seeing, more meaning than he can draw out of the phrase *make it work*. For seven years his eyes have been seeing in a different light. The light of the outside is different, less focused and cast everywhere, and his mind is playing catch-up.

Think of me as an ordained social worker, the man in denim laughs.

The front door swings open and two boys no older than sixteen stride in with purpose. From his seat he can tell that the boy covering the door is abnormally tall and lanky. The other boy is taking the lead, striding up to the counter with one hand on a piece that's half-tucked and the other slamming on the counter.

Yo, Papi, you know what's up, goes the lead boy.

They're sloppy, he notices. Just children. Still, his nerves react as if he is still on the inside. Without realizing what he's doing he's swung one leg out from his seat to clear the table, and he's readied his fork, which he hadn't used up until now because he used his hands to eat the Italian hot dog. He's subtle, though, and the boys don't even notice.

The man in denim is casual, pivots in the seat and swings

an arm over the back. Hey, Joseph, he calls out to the lead boy.

Joseph acknowledges the man in denim before firing off one last threat that lands somewhere behind the counter. Then Joseph adds to the man in denim, I ain't know you was in here.

When Joseph looks at him, sees his half-rising stance, the fork in his hand, he feels exposed before the boy. He's afraid for an instant, not of the conflict, he's ready for that, but of being discovered for what he is: a convict who should be locked up, someone afraid of the outside.

Yeah, I'm eatin here with somebody, says the man in denim. C'mon over here. And bring your tall friend with you. Is that Al-rahim? Goddamn, boy, you a lanky thing.

Al-rahim nods. Joseph's the talker.

Roach know y'all down here?

Nah, Joseph answers. We was just ridin through, you know.

Well, this ain't a good spot for y'all to play.

I got you.

I won't say nothin, the man in denim adds, but I don't wanna see y'all down here again. This my jurisdiction.

The boys agree reluctantly, but they're had. They look so young, he thinks again, and they leave but they slam the door on the way out. An unnamed rattling hangs in the air.

The man in denim turns back to him as if nothing happened, as if to pick up the conversation again after reaching for the salt or a napkin. Oh, yeah, the man in denim adds, And you gotta come to my church every week. For appearances, you know?

Appearances.

Yeah, but we can talk about that later. You figure it out, though.

As they get up to leave he registers who is behind the

counter. He'd been so overwhelmed when he entered that he hadn't really noticed. There's a twenty-something kid holding either a broom or a mop, he can't tell, and there's another the same age working the grill. There's also a frail gray beard with glasses who slides a paper bag across the counter toward the man in denim. Thank you, the gray beard says.

The man in denim plays coy, feigns with a hand to his chest and says, That's not, no. Please. It's what anyone else would do.

But the gray beard insists, Please. A donation. For your church.

The man in denim finally accepts: God thanks you.

You do his work, the gray beard says mechanically and without conviction.

Then the two of them are in the car again and the man in denim is running through the itinerary for the day. First, we gonna visit some brothers from the church. To acclimate you.

Outside the passenger side window the city is dirty and gritty in a way that feels more real than the bleached and sterilized spaces he's known for the last seven years. He spots crushed coffee cups and crumpled paper ditched along the sidewalk and while at a stop light something that looks like a used condom leans against the curb. A feeling comes back to him, a feeling he hasn't felt in a long time. It's the city. The city is bringing it out again. He can't explain why, but he wants to pick up with his hands all of the trash on the sidewalks, all of the city's discarded wrappers and used condoms and half-dried dog turds. He wants to pull it all close, to his chest, to be near it again. Alive. But he's in this car and the city is just the background, no more real than his memory. The excitement subsides with his awareness, though understanding trails. He thinks maybe a shower would be better. Wash away the remnants of life inside. Clean his skin. Start fresh. A mercy.

He goes, So, you knew those kids at Jimmy Buff's?

Oh, the man in denim says. Yeah. I work with at-risk kids, too.

I see.

Al and JoJo. Highly motivated. Kids like that need someone to channel that energy in the right direction for 'em.

They two of Roach's boys?

You been locked up inside, you know how it is. Inside or out, everybody work for Roach.

They listened to you, though.

They got good hearts, those two. They don't mean no harm.

I got you.

They're driving. The man in denim probes some more: Where you say you grow up, again?

I didn't say.

Don't start that shit again, the man in denim says. I ain't gonna warn you no more. You either wanna be outside or you want back in.

He looks at the man in denim and abides. Summer Ave, he says.

Aight.

Mom worked at the airport.

They alive?

Who?

Your folks.

Mom's dead.

Sorry.

Yeah, me too.

How long?

Four years.

May she rest in peace.

Yeah.

The man in denim pauses before the next question. A

matter of etiquette. And your father?

A mechanic at that oil change spot on Bloomfield Ave.

He still there?

Don't know. Ain't spoke since I went in. Probably in Florida at this point. He got family down there.

The Caprice pushes through the city leaving corners in its wake. Potholes and manhole covers and other kinds of imperfections announce their existence against the body of the car or cause the man in denim to swerve away from their gravity. The blocks breathe like living things, some busier than others with eyes that come and go, feet that pound the pavement, and in the car they are like visitors at a museum exhibit of a time that is long lost but never actually went extinct. The streets are different from how he remembers them but not really. Maybe just the details. He thinks he can learn to read them again. Quick, too. Young cats are inexperienced and he knows so much. He knows what to do with his hands, how to handle and deal with situations. He knows the pinch and the pitch. He knows the dirt, and the grime never gave him pause. He knows so many things he learned long ago that he didn't forget, only reinforced through the years, and while he needs to get his street cardio up to speed even the last seven years have taught him lessons.

They pull up to the old Victorian mansion at the top of Court St on MLK Boulevard. The man in denim puts the car in park and announces, We here.

Two men sit on the steps outside the front door. Signs crowd the lawn: *All Are Welcome Here* and *Only You Can Free Yourself* and *Change Starts With You*.

He recognizes the place. He remembers it being boarded up from the time he was a child. Right here? he asks.

Yeah, the man in denim points.

He goes, Wasn't this shit closed for years?

Yeah, it's the old Krueger Mansion. Krueger-Scott, actually. City lets us use it as part of an agreement. We maintain it. It's ours now, kinda. So long as we look after it. The man in denim pulls the door handle and says, C'mon.

He thinks he recognizes one of the faces on the steps and stares longer than normal as he approaches and then passes.

The man in denim pushes inside and says, Oh yeah, and I forgot to mention, I think you might know some of the brothers.

From where? He's racing through his mind to place the face he just recognized on the steps.

Around. Everybody here city people.

He understands and remembers where he's seen the face before.

The mansion is mostly restored inside. Odd remodeling projects are still underway in various rooms, and he notices the railing and wainscoting along the stairs leading up to the second floor as well as the ceilings in the rooms that flow through wide doorways adorned with detailed woodwork. The experience of walking through is like traveling back in time. He's never seen anything like it. After the grayish whiteness that have colored his last seven years the mansion's colors and detail overwhelm his eyes. It's too much and he thinks only of how much he's not taking in.

At the end of the hallway the man in denim slides open a set of dark oak pocket doors and steps into an office with matching built-in book shelves. Close 'em, the man in denim orders without breaking stride.

As he pulls the doors to he peers down the hallway they just traversed hoping to get one last bit of visual information he can digest later but the colors and the wood and the ceilings are all calling at once and he can't make anything of anything.

Sit, sit, goes the man in denim, and then the man in denim is parked on a black leather throne of an office chair on the other side of an oak desk that is big enough to suggest that maybe the room was built around it. There are two burgundy and gold guest chairs facing the desk and a small love seat off to the right. The room is small, he notices, but it feels spacious. Maybe it's the two large windows behind the desk letting in all that natural light. He opts for the couch and tries to make out the lettering on the spines of some of the volumes on the nearest shelf. Nearly all of the books are hardcovers, the pages a pastel yellow that suggests they are neither new nor fakes.

I know that's what you thinkin, the man in denim says. They real. You can open 'em, too.

The man in denim works a desk phone, listens to some messages and takes some notes. The man in denim pulls a ledger from one of the desk drawers and makes some scribbles.

He looks at the man in denim and at the books and at the pattern on the area rug, burgundy and gold to match the guest chairs, and waits for what's next. The scene feels staged, in some ways, like a performance. He understands. He waits.

The man in denim um's and ah's while flipping through the pages in the ledger.

There's a knock on the door and the man in denim responds, Yeah.

The doors slide open and in walks another face he recognizes, except this one has a name. It's Carlos, and he knows Carlos from his time inside and from the streets before then, but Carlos doesn't acknowledge him. Carlos looks at him but walks straight to the desk and hands some envelopes to the man in denim.

Carlos says, Mail. There's somethin in there from the mayor's office, too.

Oh, really?

Yeah, it's the yellow one.

Carlos, you know this man, right?

Carlos looks at him again and then back at the man in denim and goes, Yup.

The man in denim flips through the envelopes and then, with the envelopes failing to catch his interest, tosses them all in a drawer along with the ledger.

Think he can come with us today? the man in denim asks.

It's your call.

I think he can.

If you say he's good he's good.

Aight, then, give us a minute.

They speak of him as if he's not there. He watches Carlos exit the room and then hears the man in denim ask, You and Carlos ok, right?

He goes, Yeah.

Good. Carlos is a graduate of my program. A success story, really. I think he can be a good influence on you.

I see.

There will be more here that you... recognize.

Ok.

I'm tellin you that now 'cuz though you recognize 'em you won't know 'em. Not really. They not the same men so it's really just a face you recognize. The man in denim pauses to let that sink in. And these men, they've committed to our program. Like, really committed. They appreciate what we done for 'em, as one day you gonna be for what we will do for you. So what I'm sayin is you gotta be ready 'cuz they gonna come check you.

I'm used to it.

Good. 'Cuz they gonna come see if you committed. 'Cuz this is important to 'em. This matters.

I understand.

So long as we clear. You be ready now.

The man in denim stands and so he stands. The man

135

in denim says, C'mon, and leads him through the house again, doubling back, and there are more faces he recognizes. There's Beef, who he's known since high school and who nods at him but leaves it at that, and Larry, who used to play basketball, and RJ, but these last two give him the same treatment he got from Carlos. Then they're outside again and the man in denim is pointing at parts of the property, hollering out tasks and directions to half a dozen men scattered across the lawn and the porch and the side of the mansion.

They get back in the car. The man in denim is driving the Caprice and he's in the passenger seat and Carlos and Larry are in the backseat and they're all four riding through the city. There are more empty lots than he remembers, places where people used to live.

City look different to you? Carlos asks.

It's a second before he realizes the question is addressed to him. Yeah, he answers eventually, but the delay denies his response of any conviction.

What you notice most?

No houses, he says, pointing at a fenced lot with a Buy It Now sign. He doesn't recognize the name of the real estate company.

Yeah, outside change a lot while you locked up.

He agrees. Time passed so slowly for him inside and seemingly so quickly for the city outside that it's almost as if there are two different times, one for the inside and one for the outside.

I had one memory of it, he says, so when I thought of gettin out it was always of gettin out to that image of the outside. But now it's different so it still don't really feel like I'm out.

That's the hardest thing about people askin how long you been locked up, Larry chimes in. 'Cuz it's like, time for us ain't the same, you know. You say ten years to someone out here and they look at you like it's a long time but it ain't a long time for them like it was for you, you know?

That's why you gotta make up for lost time when you get out here, the man in denim says to close the conversation.

They pull up to a small grocery store on West Kinney. The man in denim puts the car in park but leaves the engine running. Carlos goes inside and comes out a few minutes later with a small paper bag that looks like it's holding a sandwich.

They're riding again, this time to a laundromat and then riding again to a liquor store and then to another grocery store and then a carwash and a bakery. Each stop produces another paper bag. All small businesses. The Caprice doesn't stop at any of the large supermarkets or pharmacy chains.

It's an hour later and they've been cruising through the city. Six stops. He's counted. A scenic tour, of sorts.

Someone got shot on Walnut this mornin, the man in denim says.

Yeah, Larry adds, I heard.

Over a cell phone. Shame. We know who did it?

No, Carlos answers, but we will soon. Kids, is my guess.

We should send somebody to see the family.

I take care of it, Carlos says.

They pull up in front of a go-go bar and the man in denim puts the car in park and turns calmly to him and says, Ok, now it's your turn.

My turn to what? he asks, but he knows.

The man in denim becomes paternal. Just walk up to the bar and say that you here to pick up the donation. They know.

Carlos and Larry are statues in the back. They may not be breathing from what he can tell.

Who do I talk to? he asks.

Anyone behind the bar.

But they don't know who I am.

Don't matter.

I could be anyone. I could be an impostor.

The man in denim chuckles: No one would do that.

And then he's out of questions. He wants to delay some more but now he can hear Carlos and Larry finally breathing in the back and he knows this is what it means to make it work.

As if prompted the man in denim goes, You gonna make this work or what?

Yeah.

So go make it work.

But... it's just that...

Go on, now. We be right here.

And then he's doing it. He gets out of the car and slides into the bar. He hopes no one on the street has seen him because he doesn't want to be identified later, if it comes to that. The bar takes up practically the entire space so as soon as he walks inside he's belly up. The place isn't deep but it's long, stretching out nearly in full to his right. It's dark, with lights focused on the stage and bar. There are two stragglers, former construction worker types, old heads with dirty fingers wrapped around their beer mugs, and a dancer on the stage that he tries to avoid so he can focus. She's facing the other way, anyway, and that's fine. He reminds himself to breathe and he wipes his palms on his sides but a bartender approaches him and she's in a black top with her arms and shoulders exposed and her hair is up in the back so that he can see the coastline of her neck. He tastes salt in his mouth as she smiles and asks, What can I get you, handsome?

He's petrified. He wants to grab her face and squeeze away her pretty little smile that makes him feel small. He steels himself and stares at her but he can't speak just yet. He needs a moment, but then a moment is gone and she's still waiting for an answer.

She makes a face and goes, Can I...

The donation.

What? She chuckles. She looks amused, puts a bar napkin in front of him. He's standing and clutching the rim around the bar harder than he'd realized and she has noticed but not yet processed.

I want the donation. Then, softer, a revision: I'm here for the donation.

Her eyes go big and she says, Oh, ok. Lemme run in the back. She turns and goes and he makes it a point not to drop his eyes to follow her leaving for fear it will sink him into the ground where he stands.

He's there and the dancer is making her way to him on the stage now, he can sense her approach, and he looks up and it's not as bad as he thought. She's exotic but not beautiful. Her eyes are too far apart and something about the height of the stage and the bar and bottles between them makes their interaction less than real and he feels no draw to her. He wishes he could deal with her instead of having to control himself around the bartender with the neck and the shoulders and the hair. The dancer drops her ass and gyrates her hips to gauge his interest. She's serious, nimble on thin heels. He keeps staring like looking into the darkness at the bottom of a well. He sees nothing and the dancer understands and slithers her way back to the other end of the stage.

The bartender exits into the bar from a door across the way and he watches her walk all the way back to him. The fire returns, burning deeper as she approaches, because the bartender comes close and makes eye contact again and she's not afraid of him or his thoughts. He can tell she knows his kind.

Here you go, she says handing him a paper bag like all the other paper bags he's seen today. You come back some other time, ok, just to visit.

He snatches her face in his right hand, pulls her in a few inches until he realizes she's not pulling back. Her skin is soft but she's not frail. She doesn't flinch. He doesn't squeeze, just watches her stillness. Then he lets her go, no remorse in his eyes. She looks at him. No blink. Still not afraid. He hears the music playing for the first time.

He turns his back and pushes through the door to the outside. The afternoon brightness is nearly blinding and he tries to breathe again. One foot on the first step and the other on another and then his mouth is dry and he's motionless in full view of the world. He spots a patrol car at his two o'clock, riding the opposite way the Caprice is facing. He drops the paper bag before he knows what he's done. He doesn't hear it hit the ground as much as he feels its dry smack on the sidewalk. Then his brain catches up to what his eyes are processing and he realizes that the cops in the patrol car aren't even looking in his direction, that they're talking unaware of him, though he watches them go all the way past. From inside the Caprice, Carlos is staring at him. He picks up the bag but has to focus to land his trembling hand in the right place. He finds it on the third try. Then two attempts before he locates the door handle.

The man in denim is making notes in a green moleskine notebook and there isn't a sound from the back seat as he stares straight ahead and places the paper bag in the seat between himself and the man in denim.

The man in denim closes the notebook and slides it into the left jacket pocket. Then the man in denim takes the paper bag and squeezes it for measure.

Yeah, the man in denim laughs and nods, you gonna make it work just fine.

Hugo dos Santos is a Luso-American writer, editor, and translator. He is the author of *Then, there*, a collection of Newark stories published by Spuyten Duyvil, and the translator of *A Child in Ruins*, the collected poems of José Luís Peixoto, published by Writ Large Press and a staff pick at the Paris Review Daily. Hugo has been awarded fellowships by the MacDowell Colony and the Disquiet International Literary Program. His work has been nominated for the Pushcart Prize and won a Write Well Award, and has appeared or is forthcoming in Barrelhouse, Electric Literature, Hobart, Puerto del Sol, The Common, The Fanzine, and elsewhere. Hugo is a co-founder of the Brick City Collective and is associate editor at DMQ Review.